A page from Lorna Willow's datebook...

TO DO

○
○ **MONDAY**
○   (first day of work)

Dinner with Joe

~~TV~~ 8:00   (babysitter cancelled)
Clint agrees to baby sit

TUESDAY

Date with Clyde Simmons
(The Canasta King)
B-O-R-I-N-G!!

Clint saves the day again!

WEDNESDAY

~~Stu Littleman~~ No-sHOW
(a mildew allergy??)

○ Movies
○   with Clint ♡
○

Dear Reader,

Oh no—dating! It's something I actually have to think about, just like a lot of women. And so far the men I've run into seem to have a lot more in common with Clyde Canasta than Mr. Right. "Who's Clyde Canasta?" you ask. He's a character from Renee Roszel's first Yours Truly novel, *Brides for Brazen Gulch*. Luckily— for you and for heroine Lorna Willow—he's *not* the hero of the book. That would be Clint McCord. Now *he's* a date I could deal with!

Of course, after dating comes (maybe) marriage. Unless you're Cheri Weatherwax, heroine of Lori Herter's *Blind-Date Bride*. In that case marriage— and a million bucks—comes first, but if dating your husband were really like this, I think more couples would meet at the altar and take it from there. Check out this latest in her MILLION-DOLLAR MARRIAGES miniseries to see what I mean.

And don't forget to come back next month for two more books about unexpectedly meeting, dating... and marrying Mr. Right.

Enjoy!

Leslie Wainger
Senior Editor and Editorial Coordinator

Please address questions and book requests to:
Silhouette Reader Service
U.S.: 3010 Walden Ave., P.O. Box 1325, Buffalo, NY 14269
Canadian: P.O. Box 609, Fort Erie, Ont. L2A 5X3

RENEE ROSZEL

Brides for Brazen Gulch

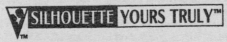

Published by Silhouette Books

America's Publisher of Contemporary Romance

SILHOUETTE BOOKS

ISBN 0-373-52026-3

BRIDES FOR BRAZEN GULCH

About the author

RENEE ROSZEL is the bestselling author of eighteen romance novels. *Brides for Brazen Gulch* is her first Yours Truly, and it's typical of her quirky style—not unlike the story's heroine, Lorna, who's a little south of normal herself.

Renee never set out to be a nonconformist or quirky, and neither did Lorna. But some people just have a talent for it. Like getting the hiccups in church.

And like Lorna, Renee is a sucker for animals. She even rescues spiders and wasps from the house and sets them free. She says she feels just a little bad that one of those wasps stung her husband right between the eyes. She asks that we keep her propensity for rescuing wasps just between us. Her hubby might not be thrilled to hear it, considering—well, you know.

Besides residing in a haven for ungrateful insects, Renee lives with her husband (until he reads this), a precious mutt named Macho, and a crippled cat with an attitude. Renee's two sons also love animals and have been known to rescue wasps for their mom. (This, too, should be kept just between us.)

Renee hopes you enjoy Lorna's unorthodox tumble into true love with hunky Clint McCord. And speaking of love, she *loves* to hear from her fans. You can write her at: PO Box 700154, Tulsa, Oklahoma, 74170

To my brother, Rik "Barney-Parney-Poo" Roszel,
Another "Andy Griffith Show" nut
who, like his big sis, loves
"Mayberry—Gateway to Danger!"

1

Wanted: Nurse, Plumber, Librarian and Hardware Store Manager. Prefer single women not averse to the idea of matrimony. Send résumés to the city council of Brazen Gulch, Texas—headquarters of the Brazen Backhoe Company—where there are two men for every woman.

"Am I on fire?"

Lorna snapped around to locate the person who'd made that smart-aleck remark. A tall man was lounging against the doorjamb of a redbrick building. He was staring in her direction, over the head of Brazen Gulch's stout mayor. As she jumped down from the truck cab, she decided nobody with such a smart mouth deserved to be *that* good-looking.

When she next looked up, he was scanning her refurbished fire engine, even though Brazen Gulch's mayor was talking to him. As the man stared, his lips parted in a grin. Both his smirk and his sarcastic remark irked her. Her truck wasn't even *red*, for heaven's sake. True, it had fought fires years ago, but after she bought it, at a goodwill auction, she'd painted it a tasteful cornflower blue— obviously *not* a fire-fighting color. She had half a mind to catch the mayor's eye and tell him to forget the whole thing. She could sleep in the truck if she had to.

"Should I get out, Mom?" Her son's question brought her back to the present, and she took a deep breath, counting to ten. There was Sam to consider, after all. Moving to Brazen Gulch was supposed to give her son a better life, not make him a homeless vagrant.

She nodded. "Sure, honey. Hop out." From out of nowhere, their pet squirrel, Barney Fife, leaped onto her arm and scampered to perch on her head, one of his favorite spots. Lorna sighed, scooping him off and planting him on her shoulder. "Oh, no, you don't. I have a feeling that's where the term *squirrelly* came from."

They needed a place to stay, and when a favor was needed, putting one's best foot forward was the accepted mode of behavior—which in some circles might include hiding the wild animals.

But sooner or later, whoever took them in would have to find out about their odd pets. She felt a surge of inadequacy. All she wanted was a normal, average life, so why couldn't she manage to own a dog or a cat, like everybody else?

"Barney, stay on my shoulder and pretend you're a parrot," she muttered, shutting her door and walking to Sam's side of the truck. "We might as well let this guy in on all the bad news. Go ahead and get Aunt Bee out of the back. It's too hot in mid-July to leave her in the truck."

Sam reached behind the seat and got his hedgehog's cage, carefully maneuvering it out. Lorna tried to calm herself by taking in the scenery. The mayor had told her this was a flying school. That was obvious, seeing as there was a single-engine plane sitting on a runway beside a metal airplane hangar.

In front of that was the two-story brick structure where the mayor and the stranger were conversing. Beside the front door stood an apple tree, giving the place an unexpectedly homey appeal. All it needed was a tire swing and a couple of barefoot boys clambering in its branches.

She'd loved her first glimpse of Brazen Gulch. It had looked just like Mayberry—maybe it was a little flatter and with fewer trees, but it was a quaint, charming place. Just the sort of town she'd dreamed it would be. With the lightning damage in what was to have been her apartment, they weren't off to a perfect start, but surely things would be fine in the long run.

When she reached her son's side, Barney had sprawled on her shoulder like a furry epaulet, whipping his tail back and forth and scolding sternly in her ear. He hadn't liked being uprooted from Dallas, and he'd made it clear by chewing her road map to shreds. They were lucky they'd managed to find their way to the tiny West Texas community at all.

Absentmindedly smoothing her overalls, she murmured, "Try to look normal."

"Huh?"

Sam's expression was pinched in confusion. Her heart filling with love, she smiled at him. She adored her son, and wanted badly to give him the secure life he deserved.

Taking his chin in her fingers, she murmured, "Nothing, honey. You're perfect." He smiled back and took his mother's hand. She squeezed reassuringly. "We'll be fine. Even if this guy doesn't want us. We'll get by." Wishing she felt as sure as she pretended to, she tugged him forward.

Even from twenty feet away, Lorna could hear what Mayor Coffee was explaining, about the fire-damaged apartment over the plumbing office and how it would take two or three weeks to repair. He lowered his voice to a confidential whisper, and her cheeks grew hot. She was sure he was reminding the man that Brazen Gulch needed both a plumber *and* marriageable women and it was his civic duty to help out in this emergency.

The stranger's glance lifted again, to scan the newcomers heading his way. Apparently Barney caught his eye, and that cocky grin bloomed once more. Lorna met his gaze and bravely held it. She'd stared down others who looked upon her as quirky—not crazy, mind you, but someone a bit south of normal. Sometimes, because of her soft heart, her good intentions went awry, making her *seem* a little peculiar. That was all.

She lifted her chin, refusing to be cowed by his amused stare. Barney skittered around, his tail curling about her jaw. Not caring to look like Abraham Lincoln at the moment, she swept the fluff aside, managing to hold on to her poise. There was nothing wrong with taking in an orphaned squirrel. She didn't need to be embarrassed. Let him stare.

Mayor Coffee was a stout man, five foot six, exactly Lorna's height. The stranger was almost a foot taller, lean, with massive shoulders that virtually blocked his doorway. He appeared to have hastily thrown on his cotton shirt, for it was unbuttoned, showing off an indecent view of lightly haired chest.

He crossed his arms before him, masking his belly. Even so, she'd glimpsed enough to know it was washboard-solid, like those pictured on the Tough Tummy exercise tapes she'd long ago given away in despair. Apparently there were those who succeeded where she failed.

He wore jeans in the current baggy style, but she had a feeling he had the legs of an athlete hidden under that denim. Probably had a Tight Thighs and Cute Calves exercise tape he used religiously. Interestingly, he was barefoot. She wondered if somewhere inside the building there was a naked woman waiting, miffed at being interrupted in midforeplay.

It would seem so, judging by his mussed hair, black wisps falling across his forehead. He lifted an eyebrow as he watched her approach. She gave a forced smile, not sure whether it was for Sam's sake or possibly out of self-consciousness about his coitus interruptus.

He was watching her as thoroughly as she was watching him. Something about his unwavering look bothered her. His eyes, the same dark color as his hair, were compelling, even in an incredulous squint. But it was his mouth that really bothered her. Oh, there was nothing wrong with it. On the contrary. It was a gorgeous, masculine mouth— as gorgeous, masculine mouths went. She just didn't like the curl of amusement that constantly rode his lips. *He was laughing at her, the bum!* She had a feeling he did that a lot—that he took very little seriously.

Maybe she should feel better knowing that. Maybe he would have laughed even if she strolled up in a navy three-piece suit and sensible heels, with nary a quadruped on her person. But she didn't feel better. As a matter of fact, she disliked that about a man—the inability to take things seriously.

Putting up her guard, she once again brushed Barney's tail from her chin, preparing for this half-dressed, smirking Adonis to tell her to hit the road and look elsewhere to house her menagerie. To be honest, she wasn't upset at the prospect. Let him get back to playing sex games with his girlfriend and aim his impertinent grin in another direction. *And the sooner the better.*

"Mrs. Willow, this is Clint McCord. As I told you, he's kinda new to Brazen Gulch himself, and runs a flying school here." The mayor turned toward the man. "Clint, this is Mrs. Lorna Willow, our new plumber, and her boy, Sam.''

Clint's glance roamed from Lorna's chattering squirrel to Sam, to Aunt Bee, rolled in a prickly ball in her wire cage, then back to Lorna's face. He gave her a slow nod. ''Afternoon, ma'am.'' Though his eyes twinkled with laughter, he didn't mention the fact that Barney was burrowing in the curls at her nape, evidently looking for nuts. She had a feeling this Clint person thought the squirrel might find some.

The mayor cleared his throat and readjusted his turquoise bolo tie. Lorna could tell he was concerned that this guy was not convinced he needed to get involved with her problems. ''I was telling Clint about the apartment fire. He was very upset to hear it.''

Lorna scanned Clint's face, searching for signs of anguish and coming up empty. ''I can see that,'' she said, deciding a roof over her head wasn't worth groveling for.

Mayor Coffee's already florid face deepened a shade but, to his credit, he didn't scowl at her. He simply smiled more broadly at the man in the doorway. ''Well . . . I was thinkin' the vacant cottage on Clint's property would be as welcome as a pat straight flush.'' His accent thick as Texas chili, he hurried on, ''And since our hotel's packed with curiosity-seeking fillies who read our ad, findin' a free room in Brazen Gulch is like tryin' to scratch your ear with your elbow.'' He lifted a hand as though to pat Clint's shoulder, then hesitated, evidently thinking better of using the good-old-boy ploy on this man. Clint McCord didn't look like the type to be manipulated by fake camaraderie to Lorna, either. ''Er...I've been tellin' Clint how bad we need a plumber in these parts, since Rusty up and retired to Florida last fall.'' He laughed self-consciously. ''I bet you could use a plumber yourself, Clint.''

The tall man gave Lorna an odd look, then grinned that bothersome grin. He didn't respond to the mayor, and Lorna decided that was for the best. She'd just bet she knew what that look meant, and it didn't have anything to do with stopped-up drains.

She dropped her gaze, though it wasn't necessary to hide his smile from her view. Barney managed that by shifting to present his hindquarters to Clint, flinging his bushy tail across her eyes. She thought the squirrel was showing good judgment in turning his back. She had the same urge.

"You really *could* use a plumber," Sam chimed in, sounding like an overeager Hollywood agent. "Old buildings like this have lousy plumbing. Lots of muck and rust. My mom can fix anything."

Lorna glanced at him, amazed by the conviction in his voice. What a great kid—so sure of her competence, however inaccurate he might be. Just then, Barney decided he'd had enough of shoulder-sitting and scrambled onto her head. She had a horrible flash of what her hair must look like—the lower half dark blond curls; the upper half red-brown and squirrel-shaped. Even so, she squared her shoulders to preserve her dignity and gave Mr. Clint McCord a *"So there"* look.

Removing the animal to her shoulder, she said tightly, "We don't want to keep you, Mr. McCord. I'm sure there's somewhere else we can stay. Don't bother yourself."

"But, Mrs. Willow . . ." The mayor put a beefy hand on her wrist, his tone desperate. Worried, protuberant eyes swung from her to the man lounging in his doorway. "I'm sure Clint, here, was about to give his consent—knowing the town's powerful *serious* need."

Barney leaped to her head again, and this time she gave up. She wasn't surprised that Clint's gaze followed the squirrel. After all, how many men met women outside the circus or a special-care home with wildlife in their hair? He watched as the squirrel dug through curls, its tail swishing like a windshield wiper before her eyes.

Fighting a grin, he glanced back at the shorter man. "The cabin isn't furnished, Jerome."

The mayor lifted his hands in a "No problem" gesture. "There's plenty of folks in town who'll be pleased to donate furniture for the cause. I'm sure they'd even give the walls a fresh swipe of paint. Why, you'd end up with a nice little piece of rental property."

Lorna's mind was screaming, *Don't beg this grinning smart mouth! I'd rather sleep in a ditch.* But she restrained herself. Sam didn't need to spend his boyhood in gutters, and Barney was terrified of being left outdoors.

Clint glanced at Lorna, indicating the squirrel with a nod. "Do the animal rights people know about your hat?"

Before she could form an answer, Sam laughed. "Barney likes to be high up. In our old apartment, he'd hide on the top shelf of our bookcase. Sometimes he'd push books out on people he didn't like."

Clint turned to the boy. "Hardback or paperback?"

Lorna was startled by his wit, and found herself fighting a grin.

"Depends," Sam said. "One of Mom's dates got our dictionary dumped on his head. The dork was unconscious for two hours."

Clint grinned again, this time displaying a slashing dimple. Suddenly everything inside her stilled. *Oh, no, don't let me be attracted to this guy!* She'd seen that sexy, devil-may-care type of grin before—on her late husband. Bill had been a wild, grab-life-by-the-tail man who should never have married. He'd taken nothing seriously, and because of it he'd died too young.

Now she knew why she'd reacted so strongly to this Clint person from the moment she saw him. He was just like Bill. Same sexy appeal. Same reckless streak. She backed away a step in unconscious self-defense.

"It's pretty hot," he was saying to Sam. "I've got some colas in the fridge. Why don't you get yourself one?"

Sam's eyes widened in happy surprise. "Cool. Thanks."

"Inside, to your left."

The boy disappeared, still lugging the cage that held Aunt Bee. Once he was gone, Clint turned to the mayor. "Jerome, if you can get the local tail chasers to fix up that cottage and furnish it, who am I to complain?"

Lorna was insulted by his bluntness, and stifled a gasp. It was no secret that the Brazen Gulch advertisement asked specifically for women to fill the vacant positions in town—women not opposed to the idea of marriage. But this guy had put it awfully crudely. Eyeing him with distaste, she muttered, "That was so charming, for a minute there I thought you were Sir Walter Raleigh."

The flash of teeth he aimed her way was unrepentant. "You'd be surprised how often I hear that."

She swept Barney's tail out of her eyes. "I'd faint dead away with shock."

"You don't look like the fainting type, Mrs. Willow," he said.

Lorna opened her mouth to retort, but couldn't think of a thing to say. *For your information, I faint all the time, Buster!* didn't seem like an appropriate comeback. As she mentally cast about for a terse response to what had smacked suspiciously of a compliment, Mayor Coffee said, "Then it's a done deal. I'll pass the word, and by tomorrow evenin' Mrs. Willow'll have a place to stay and you'll have yourself a fixed-up piece of property."

"Hey," Sam called from inside. "There's a lady in here who wants to know if you're gonna be much longer."

Clint turned as the boy reappeared with a can of cola. "Tell her to cool her jets. I'll be right there."

As Sam reentered the house with the message, Lorna's cheeks grew fiery again. Good grief! They really had interrupted—

"Is that all, then?" Clint asked the mayor.

"Well, there is this one more thing—"

"You bet there's one more thing!" Alarm and anger slithered along Lorna's spine. "Did you send my son in there where you've got a *naked* woman?"

Clint flicked her a glance, exasperation flashing in his eyes. "Don't you think he'd have mentioned it if she'd been naked?"

Her fury turned to embarrassment. She couldn't bring herself to apologize, so she took the offensive. "If you were doing what your disheveled appearance tells me you were doing, then you have some nerve calling anybody *else* a tail chaser!"

He grinned, annoying her by looking darling and cocky at the same time. "The fashion police drop by so rarely, I guess I let myself go."

His laughing eyes held hers ruthlessly. She was so angry at his refusal to give her a straight answer, she wanted to jump him bodily and slap that grin off his face—at least that was what she hoped she wanted. Maybe it was a good thing the grip of his gaze destroyed her ability to move or speak.

"Ahem." Mayor Coffee took her hand and patted it, but faced Clint. "As I was sayin', Mrs. Willow and her son don't have anywhere to spend the night tonight."

"*No!*" Lorna shouted, exploding from her stupor. Too late, she got herself under control. "I mean—we can sleep in the truck. Mr. McCord has—has company...." She couldn't bear to look directly at those sparkling eyes.

"They can bed down in the hangar. There's a bathroom out there. My company won't be here much longer." He shrugged his hands into his pockets, revealing his taut belly.

"That's a deal, then!" The mayor clapped his big paws together. "Isn't that dandy as pie, Mrs. Willow?"

Lorna chewed the inside of her cheek. She'd never felt so uncomfortable or so unwelcome in her life. But, for Sam's sake, she refused to run screaming toward the highway. "I can't express *how* I feel...."

Clint chuckled, clearly more attuned to the double entendre than Brazen Gulch's mayor. "The hangar's that big metal—"

"I know what an airplane hangar looks like."

Clint grinned her way. "I admire well-informed women."

Lorna heard the teasing tone, but refused to jump at the bait. Poor Mayor Coffee would have a stroke.

Sam came outside. "Mr. McCord, that pretty lady said you were teaching her to fly. How can you do that *inside* the building?"

Lorna closed her eyes and inhaled to hold on to her composure. "No doubt he's giving her an *oral* exam." She blanched in dismay when she realized she'd spoken her thought aloud.

Clint cleared his throat, drawing her troubled gaze. "You must leave that interesting mind of yours to science, Mrs. Willow." His grin wry, he turned to Sam. "There is a certain amount of preliminary study a student must do before he—or she—can go up in the plane. That's why she's inside."

Sam nodded, taking a drink of cola. Lorna was morti-
fied, and suddenly filled with self-doubt. Could she have
been wrong about what had been going on inside before
they arrived? Had he actually been instructing some
woman about air currents or whatever? Dubious, she
peered at her tousled host. His answering half grin didn't
tell her a darn thing.

"Well—we'll be headin' off for now, Clint, boy. And
speakin' for the folks of Brazen—"

He cut in. "No problem. If you'll excuse me, I do have
a student waiting."

Not sure what to think, Lorna spun away. She'd made
a disastrous first impression on her new landlord, which
wasn't like her at all. People might think she was a little
odd, but *never* trashy-minded. Darn the guy for reminding her of Bill and making her go a little crazy with a flood
of bittersweet memories.

Chewing the inside of her cheek, she grew dejected. Was
this serendipitous move to Brazen Gulch another case of
her good intentions gone horribly wrong?

The next morning, Lorna had been awakened when a
motorcade of bachelors arrived, all brawny and high-
spirited, willing and ready to get the cottage into shape.
July was whizzing by, and was already half-over. So much
had happened that Lorna had almost managed to put the
Clint McCord fiasco from her mind. Almost. She hadn't
seen him since she'd made a fool of herself at his front
door—or he'd made a fool of her. She still didn't know
which—*yet*. But as the day progressed, she grew more and
more tense, knowing that sooner or later he'd show up and
grin that sly grin, all the while insisting he was Saint Clint
McCord, the monkish flying teacher. Yeah. Sure!

She tossed her head, allowing the breeze to cool her nape. She was accustomed to hot weather in July, but she'd been delighted to discover that Brazen Gulch was much less humid than Dallas. The dry heat out here was a nice change. Even though the thermometer on the outside of the hangar read ninety-two degrees, it didn't seem that hot. The cavernous airplane hangar, with the breeze blowing through it, was cool even now, at midday.

She glanced around, paying little attention to the conversation, and grimaced inwardly. She'd never been in such a bizarre situation in her life as she was now, and for her that was saying a lot. She felt like a Christmas turkey, sitting there in the middle of a picnic blanket, ten local bachelors surrounding her. She knew it was crazy, but she was afraid any second somebody would shout, *"Go!"* and they'd all dive at her, grabbing for their favorite parts.

They were sitting on the grass, in the shade of the hangar, taking a lunch break. Somebody coughed, and in her stress, it sounded like a starting gun. In a knee-jerk reaction, she slapped her arms over her breasts. The men went still, no doubt startled by her violent flinch. She grimaced. "Uh...mosquito..." she lied weakly. "Got it..." Feeling foolish, she carried out her charade by pretending to flick the nonexistent insect into the grass.

As the men began recommending brands of insect repellent, her eyes and her attention strayed again. Sam was on the edge of the blanket, sound asleep, Aunt Bee nestled in the crook of his arm. She smiled at her son. So uncomplaining, so hardworking. How lucky she was to have his stabilizing influence in her life. It never ceased to amaze her that she'd been blessed with such a levelheaded kid. Must have been a mutated gene, or a throwback to some unknown levelheaded ancestor. Bill certainly hadn't carried any noticeably sensible genes. Whatever the explanation was for Sam's nature, she was thankful.

Her gaze traveled to the cottage off in the distance to her right. It made a quaint picture, situated in the midst of a field of tall grasses and nodding wildflowers. The cottage was a petite wooden structure surrounded by a white picket fence and cuddled protectively beneath the branches of an immense, leafy oak. The outside walls of the cottage and the fence had been freshly painted white. The door and window shutters were a celery green.

One of the bachelors—Ed, she believed was his name— had provided the paint. Unfortunately, the colors he'd provided inside were less conventional. The bedroom and connecting bath were as dark as a cave with a new coat of navy blue, and both the living room and the kitchen were now an eye-popping pink. She found out through conversation that the paint had been left over from a disco Ed had owned in the late seventies. Now he ran the town's gas station. She wondered if it was electric pink, too.

Her glance roved to a pickup truck, filled with donated furniture—a strange brew, from the puce Victorian couch to a knock off of an art deco dresser, painted a garish yellow. She felt a little sick, wondering if these men thought a few cans of paint or a rickety card table would make her owe them something . . . *sexual?*

She glanced at the men in panic, afraid she'd blurted that aloud. When she was satisfied the topic of conversation was still centered on insect repellents, she breathed a sigh, but was not truly relieved. What was the matter with her lately? Ever since yesterday, her thoughts had been strangely sexual.

She fought off the notion. These men were generous, caring people who'd done nothing but behave like gentlemen. She supposed the stress of the trip and paint fumes were to blame for her peculiar turn of mind.

The men joked, trying to be entertaining. She laughed in appropriate places, but was only half listening as they chattered and ate cold-cut sandwiches. She noticed movement in the distance and glanced in that direction. Her stomach lurched as the event she'd been dreading became a reality. Her disturbing host was finally making an appearance.

He was fully dressed this time, wearing a knit pullover, thigh-hugging jeans and cowboy boots. But he was still lounging, this time against the gaping hangar door. She had a surly desire to ask if his shoulders were too heavy to cart around, but she decided he'd take it as a compliment and grin that lewd grin. It bothered her to discover that he was looking at her.

He canted his head, as though telling her to join him. Her stomach fluttered again, and she didn't like it. The sensation reminded her of Bill. He'd had that same talent—a small nod or a certain look, and she would follow him anywhere. She broke eye contact and pointedly turned away. After a few seconds, she found herself getting up and excusing herself from the male throng. Barney, who'd been snoring in her lap, woke when she stirred, and leaped to her shoulder.

Accustomed to the squirrel's actions, she hardly noticed. Her gaze was riveted on the man idling before her. The noon breeze toyed with his hair like a lover's fingers. She swallowed, wondering why that particular image rushed to her mind's eye. She steeled herself, aware of her weakness for charismatic rascals. Inwardly, she vowed to remain all business, serious and aloof. Whatever he wanted probably had to do with her living accommodations. She'd listen, deal with it, ignore his grin and *go!*

"Yes?" she asked. Her voice had come out an octave high, so she swallowed several times to refine it.

He crossed his arms before his chest. "Sleep well last night?"

She was surprised by his inquiry, since he hadn't come out to check on them. When she and Sam returned after having dinner with the mayor and his wife, the last thing she'd wanted to do was see the guy. Apparently the feeling had been mutual.

She and Sam had placed their bedrolls beneath the wings of what appeared to be a World War II fighter plane and kept to themselves. Sam had fallen right to sleep. She'd tossed and turned until dawn, wondering if she'd done the right thing coming here. "We were fine, thanks." She said it as pleasantly as she could, but it still came out strained.

He grinned that lopsided grin that affected her badly, and she sensed a momentary hysteria, but tamped it down.

"Thanks for fixing the sink," he said.

She shrugged off his compliment and tried to do the same with her unease. "I can't sleep with the sound of a dripping faucet."

"Then you're in the right business."

She smiled tentatively, though it was against her will.

"Well, well . . ." He chuckled. "I see my fatal charm is finally working."

Her smile faded. It wasn't that she was irritated with him. She was more upset with herself for allowing the charm he'd so casually spoken of to affect her. She decided her best defense was to put distance between them. Emotional, as well as physical. "Mr. McCord," she began tartly, "I'm sure you're heaven's gift to single women, but I have a specific agenda here, and it does *not* include being charmed by you. Let's get that straight up front, shall we?"

He pursed his lips, regarding her thoughtfully. After a moment, his grin returned with a masculine appeal that was impossible to ignore, even though she tried her best. "I'm curious, Mrs. Willow. Why the hostility? Surely you suspected you might get hit on in a town full of bachelors. If you're that afraid of men, why did you move here?"

His candidness caught her off guard, and she couldn't form a coherent thought. "I, uh, I'm not—" she began, then lost her voice, but doggedly regained her poise. "I'm here because I'm a *plumber.* I think growing up in a small town will be good for my son. And if one day I find a nice, ordinary guy I think I could make a life with, then I *might* get married. So you see, I'm not afraid of men!"

He lifted his chin in a half nod, but it was one of those movements that said he didn't quite believe her. Irritated, she blurted, "I'm not afraid of these men. I'm just afraid of—" She cut herself off. Good grief, she'd almost said too much.

His eyes narrowed. "Of me?" He sounded incredulous. "Hell, sweetheart, I haven't laid a glove on you."

She shook herself mentally. "Not *you!*" she lied, then hissed defensively, "Boy, are you full of yourself."

Barney skittered off her shoulder and made a dive between her T-shirt and the bib of her overalls. It didn't startle her. She was used to his penchant for napping in dark, warm places, like loose pockets or under big collars. After a second, his pointed snout popped over the rim of the bib, and his wide brown eyes stared at Lorna's male companion.

Though Clint had gone serious, his eyes began to dance with mirth as they lifted from the place where Barney nestled. "I'm sorry, I seem to have lost my train of thought."

She tried not to let on, but she was more than happy to change the subject. "Look, I was thinking—since you're letting Sam and me stay here for free, I'll take a peek at your pipes—" She heard her odd word choice and quickly amended it. "I mean, I'll handle your plumbing— Er..." She frowned. That last remark was perfectly okay, but somehow, with those dusky eyes so intent on her, she felt like she'd said, *I'll swing naked on your chandelier, studmuffin.*

He ran a hand over his mouth. "I get it, Mrs. Willow. You'll repair my building's faulty plumbing in appreciation for the loan of the cabin. And you're not interested in cheap sex. Message received."

She shoved her hands in her pockets. "Good. *Fine.*" She was shaky, and reminded herself of her vow to scorn his sexy allure. Forcing her glance away, she noticed that the men were gathering up the lunch debris. "I'd better get back to work." She pivoted to go.

"Could I make one last suggestion? Purely landlord to tenant?"

She halted, and glared back. "If you can be *serious.*"

He nodded toward the squirrel in her bodice. "Allowing small animals to burrow between your breasts might give some men the wrong idea." He shrugged in a guileless-schoolboy way that was so sexy she wanted to scream. "Of course, I could be wrong. But I doubt it."

Even though he was teasing, he had a point. With a contemptuous glare, she scooped her pet out of her overalls and plopped him on her head. She supposed looking half-witted was better than looking kinky. Maybe her earlier lecherous insight hadn't been as outlandish as she thought. Maybe meaningless, easy sex was the uppermost thought in these brawny bachelors' minds.

She glowered at Clint for one additional heartbeat, then spun away, resenting the fact that he *might* have given her a piece of good advice.

2

The night was warm, and the cottage windows were thrown wide, the breeze cleansing away the last of the paint fumes. Sam was snoring softly on the Victorian couch, which was to be his bed for the next several weeks. Aunt Bee, looking like a spiky tennis ball, was asleep in her cage, on the floor by the couch. Barney sat on a card table in the kitchen area, eating the flowers the town council had given Lorna as a welcoming gift.

She sat in a green chintz chair that felt as if it had been stuffed by the Three Stooges on laughing gas. Only an inebriated comedy team could have stuffed this chair so that every curve of her body met with a coordinating lump. Somebody was probably thrilled to be rid of it.

She shifted, trying to read her horror novel. It was certainly horrible, but that was about all she could say for it. She looked over her shoulder at Barney and lifted the paperback in his direction. "Here's one you can shred for your nest, Barn. Now, since I'm giving you this, I expect you to keep your looting paws off my keeper-book box."

The squirrel halted in deflowering a shaggy chrysanthemum head and pointed his snout her way, his jowls bulging with florets. She couldn't stifle a giggle. "If Mayor Coffee could see that bouquet now, little buddy, there'd be a bounty on squirrels in Brazen Gulch."

Barney chattered at her, spewing pink petals as he scolded her. He was clearly not over his pique at their having moved away from his familiar surroundings. After all, God *didn't* rearrange the trees. "Well, it's done, Buster, so *deal* with it," she admonished.

As though insisting on having the last word, Barney ripped off the head of another mum and continued in his quest to turn the flowers into compost.

With a tired exhale, she struggled up from the lumpy chair. She didn't know why she couldn't just go to bed, but for some reason she couldn't. "I can't watch this," she muttered, deciding she might as well fix the rusty kitchen faucet. All the parts she needed were in her truck.

When she bent to kiss her son, he didn't stir. She stroked his baby-soft blond hair. Again, no sign that he knew she was there. Shaking her head, she straightened. He was so sound asleep he wouldn't wake up if his favorite heavy metal group, Dead Vipers of the Underworld, came in shrieking and bashing their guitars against the pink walls. Kids.

She was as tired as Sam, so why couldn't she rest? She didn't want to think about the reason. She told herself again that the move was the right thing to do. She had a ready-made business here, and everybody was so nice. She slipped quietly out the door, amending that. Well, almost everybody. Clint McCord's knowing grin was insidiously intimidating.

As if on cue, she heard the hum of a single-engine plane coming in low. She halted to watch as it touched down and sped along the concrete airstrip in her direction, a streak of silver in the dim moonlight.

It sailed past, stirring up a breeze. When her hair danced before her face, she came out of her trance and headed toward the parking lot and her truck. Putting the plane and its occupant from her mind, she fished around in one of the truck's exterior storage compartments to get the things she needed. On her way back, with a sack in one hand and her toolbox in her other, she blundered to a halt when confronted by Clint and a petite, giggly woman.

He surprised her by stopping. "Evening, Mrs. Willow."

She nodded. "Good evening, Mr. McCord."

She'd taken a step away when he added, "This is Audrey Peterman."

Lorna stopped again, abashed. Where had her manners gone? Nodding toward the woman, she murmured, "Hello."

The tiny woman grinned. "Hi." She stuck out a hand, then realized Lorna had no free hands to shake. "Oh—sorry. I hear you're the new plumber in town."

Lorna shifted the sack of parts under one arm and held out a hand. "Yes. And you?"

Audrey giggled and tossed her long hair. Lorna had a feeling the thick tresses were red, but she had no idea why. The light wasn't good. Audrey took Lorna's hand. "No... I'm just on a... sort of... vacation from secretarial school. Thought Brazen Gulch would be a fun place to visit."

Lorna smiled, but with effort. "I've heard it's a real tourist mecca."

The girl laughed, giving Clint a coquettish look. "Yeah, if you're a girl tourist and you like boy meccas."

Clint grinned that grin she hated—or at least *wished* she hated. She felt a sudden urge to run away. "Well, if you'll pardon me, I was about to repair a sink."

"Need help?"

Lorna was startled by Clint's offer. "No. You have... a student."

"I gotta go, anyway," Audrey said. "It's been a long day, and I'm pooped." She squeezed Clint's hands. "That was great! See you before I go back to Houston?"

He grinned at her. "Whenever you want."

With that assurance, the woman flounced away toward a compact car that had been hidden behind the fire truck. Lorna hadn't noticed it until now. At the car door, Audrey waved, then ducked in and was gone.

"I'll take the toolbox," Clint said.

She hesitated, reluctant to hand it to him. "Aren't you pooped, too?"

"Piloting a plane isn't particularly exhausting." His amused gaze ran over her from head to foot. "Or is that mind of yours jumping to conclusions again?"

Suddenly irritated with herself and her obsession with this man's sex life, she made a silent vow never to mention it or even *think* about it again. "Forget it," she muttered. "It's none of my business."

"That's true." He moved to take the toolbox again, but she avoided his touch.

"I can do it," she objected, almost desperately.

He took it from her, anyway. "Why are you working so late?"

She was startled by the question, but since he'd begun to walk toward the cottage, she hurried to keep pace with him. "I—I don't know. I can't seem to sleep—the new surroundings, I guess." Why wouldn't her brain let her rest?

"How's Sam?"

"He's smarter than I am. He's asleep."

He shifted her toolbox from one hand to the other. "This is heavy. What have you got in here, the kitchen sink?" When she gave him a *how lame* grimace, he shrugged. "I've never said that before."

"Take my advice and don't do it again."

They got to the cottage door, and she reached for the box.

"I could help."

She shook her head. "Sam's asleep on the couch."

His expression grew quizzical. "If we need a chaperon, there's always dive-bombing Barney."

She couldn't help but smile at the mental picture that conjured up. "Too bad I don't have any bookshelves."

He took hold of the doorknob. "That's the best news I've heard all day."

Before she knew it, he was standing in her pink living room. It didn't surprise her when he abruptly halted and stared. "Hell. It looks like a brothel."

She couldn't disagree. "That should make interviewing for renters fun. Question one—do you own a red rubber garter belt, madam?"

He chuckled. "I can't wait to hear question two."

She blushed at her insane turn of mind. "I'm sure you'll think of something."

"I don't know. That garter belt thing wouldn't have occurred to me."

His teeth flashed in that dratted grin—as charming and reckless as it was exciting—and the fact that it moved her at all made her grit her teeth. "Don't you have a student coming in the morning?" She hoped he'd take the hint and go.

He walked into the kitchen area, which took only four long strides. "First lesson's at nine. It's ten o'clock now, and I only need five hours of sleep."

Dismay flooded through her at the discovery that he didn't take hints well. "Don't give me too much information. It'll spoil it for me when your autobiography comes out." Reluctantly, she followed him.

He glanced her way, his grin still in place, but he didn't respond. Setting the toolbox on the card table, he noticed the scattering of bent and chewed greenery. Barney was gone, but he'd left a few mutilated petals scattered among the frayed and broken flowers. Clint picked up a stem. The top portion swung drunkenly from a spot that had been nibbled almost in two. He glanced at her, eyebrows knit. "I'd say our florist has gone off of his medication again."

She was so surprised by his joke that she grinned, then caught herself and spun away toward the sink. Hadn't she already learned the insanity of falling for an easygoing, sexy rogue? Hadn't she specifically moved to Brazen Gulch to find a stable, normal home life? She'd hoped she'd find a father for Sam—someone who'd be a reliable male role model. How crazy could guys be who manufactured backhoes?

But *this* guy didn't build earth-moving equipment. Oh, she had a feeling Clint McCord had a talent for making the earth move—unfortunately. The experience would be wondrous, but fleeting. Men like him made chaos of the lives of those who loved them.

According to what she'd heard since she'd gotten here, Clint not only taught flying lessons, he was a barnstorming pilot who took dangerous dares at air shows on the weekends. That was all she needed in her life! Another crazy daredevil! Just to be absolutely sure she was right, she faced him, demanding, "What about you?"

He'd glanced at the sink, but at her query, he looked back questioningly. "Am I on medication?"

She shook her head, feeling silly that she'd lost the thread of the conversation. "No, I meant, are you one of the bachelors planning to find a bride among the women flooding Brazen Gulch? You seem to have plenty of candidates parading through here."

"No. I'm not looking." A smile still rode his lips, but his eyes had gone flat. Clearly, marriage wasn't his favorite topic.

She lifted her chin in a half nod. Well, it was out now. She'd been right. At least he was kinder than Bill had been. At least he didn't marry his women, give them babies, then die on them in selfish, thoughtless haste.

He shrugged his hands into his pockets. "What made you ask?"

She decided to be truthful. "I just wanted to prove something to myself."

"And did you?"

"Yes." She turned away. "I'm sure your decision is best."

"Thanks." He sounded a little confused. "I guess."

She went to the sink, trying to get her mind on her work.

"So, what do you want me to do?" He sounded very close. She could smell his woodsy after-shave, and an imprudent flurry in her stomach made her panic.

"I—I really would prefer that you go." Forcing herself, she faced him, but quickly regretted it. He was barely a foot away. Grabbing the sink, she curled her fingers into the scarred porcelain, arching away from his nearness.

He was frowning in confusion, studying her, plainly wondering where her animosity had come from.

"*Please.*" She clutched so hard a nail broke, but she hardly noticed. She was rabidly renewing her vow to remain indifferent to this man.

His silence and his unwavering gaze agitated her. Just when she didn't think she could stand it any longer, he placed the broken stem he'd been holding on the counter. "No problem, Mrs. Willow." With a nod and a crooked little smile, he ambled to the door and left.

* * *

Monday morning, Lorna was making her first breakfast in her borrowed cottage. A knock at the door sent a slither up her spine. Who could possibly be coming by at seven o'clock but Clint McCord?

"I'll get it, Mom." Sam jumped up from the table, grabbing a piece of toast as he hurried to open the door. Lorna didn't even have to turn around. Sam's delighted "Hi" was all she needed to hear. It was Clint. Sam was obviously taken with the man. "Mom!" he shouted. "It's Mr. McCord!"

Straightening her shoulders, she freshened her determination to find him completely uninspiring. Taking the skillet of scrambled eggs off the butane flame, she wiped her fingers on the hand towel that served as a makeshift apron. "Is anything wrong?"

"Everything's fine." She could hear solid footfalls, and knew he'd entered the room. When she came around the corner and saw him, backlit by the rising sun, her breath caught. He looked like Mr. West Texas Cowboy, so broad-shouldered in a striped Western shirt, so slim-hipped in formfitting jeans. He had on a pair of roper boots, too. All that was missing was a ten-gallon hat.

She decided it would have been a shame to cover that splendid head of hair. Never quite tamed, dark strands of the stuff caressed his wide brow.

"Nice day." He grinned, scruffing Sam's blond mop of hair. Clearly, the man was a morning person. And he smelled good, too. Some kind of spicy-woodsy after-shave wafted across the air to her. Nice. "It seems Brazen Gulch's plumbing is in ruins," he said as she guiltily inhaled. "You've had fifteen phone messages already today from residents who are evidently dog-paddling around in their leaky houses." He handed Sam the stack of notepaper. "It's interesting how they all seem to be men." Though Clint's face was in shadow, she knew his eyes were twinkling.

She gritted her teeth against any temptation to be captivated by the charm he scattered so freely—like feed to starved cattle. "I'm sorry you were disturbed," she said. Hurrying to her son, she took the notes, scanning them. From what she could see, nothing looked urgent. She supposed she should have expected something like this— men making plumbing excuses to meet her. "From now on, I'll make sure to pass the word to call here only if it's a real emergency. These could have been left on the machine at the office."

He nodded. "Well, I've got a student coming in a few minutes." He pivoted to go.

"I thought you said your first was at nine."

He glanced back, grinned, and her heart fluttered stupidly. "You weren't the only one getting calls this morning, Mrs. Willow."

"Want some breakfast?" Sam asked, startling Lorna.

She realized she'd been rude, especially since he'd been acting as her unpaid secretary this morning. "Oh—yes, would you like a cup of coffee, at least?" It came out feebly, and she had a feeling he could sense that she didn't want him to stay.

He cocked his head, seeming to consider her request. "Maybe just a cup." His grin was easy, without a trace of slyness. And that made her even more suspicious. How dare he hang around looking so darling!

"Great!" Sam took Clint's hand and tugged him toward the table. "Have some eggs, too. Mom always makes too much food."

Though despondent over this turn of events, Lorna tried to hide her feelings. "He means my cooking's so bad, hardly any of it gets eaten."

She was caught by surprise when Clint didn't take a seat at the table, but headed for the coffee maker. "I'll just have a little caffeine."

"Coward." Her cheeks flamed, and she was appalled at herself for teasing him. Some people might have suggested that *teasing* was another word for *flirting*.

He poured coffee into a mug. "Is that a dare, Mrs. Willow?" His eyes were twinkling with blatant sex appeal. "I take dares for a living. And just between us, the game is fixed. You can't win."

Turning abruptly away, she dished out her own eggs, and was upset to note that the serving spoon shook in her fingers. He was right, and they weren't even talking about the same thing—*or were they?* Irritated at herself, she dropped the eggs back into the skillet. "On second thought, I'd better get to work. From all the phone messages, it sounds like I'm going to have a busy day." She avoided Clint's eyes as she undid the hand towel at her waist. "Sam, honey, hurry and finish. You'll have to go with me until I can find a sitter."

"Aw, Mom. I'm not a baby. Me and Barney and Aunt Bee will be fine."

"I'll be here if he needs anything," Clint said.

Lorna threw him a dubious look. "I thought you had students all morning. Won't your attention be—be diverted?" It was the least accusatory word she could come up with for what her mind was picturing—visions she'd promised herself she wouldn't even think.

He sipped coffee, watching her over the rim of the cup, his dark eyes narrowing as he computed her ill-disguised message. When he lowered the mug, his lips quirked.

"Mrs. Willow, your continued faith in my character is heartwarming." He sat his coffee mug on the wooden counter. "Sam, I could use some part-time cleanup help in the hangar while I'm in the office with my student. That way, I'll have some free time this afternoon, so you, me, Goober and Gomer can play video games at my place." He gave Lorna a completely unfair grin, then said in a taunting tone, "Okay, *Mom?*"

"Killer!" Sam shouted. "See, Mom! Mr. McCord knows I'm not a baby."

"And tomorrow my mechanic gets back. He's finally out on bail on those child-molesting charges, so he can baby-sit, too."

She gaped, shocked out of her mind.

He took another sip of coffee, then chuckled at her expression of horror. "Kidding. He was visiting his boys in California."

She shot him a "You're so funny" glare, then faced her son, smiling weakly. "You won't wander off? You don't know what sort of wild animals or rotting mine shafts there might be around here."

"Thousands," Clint said. "There might even be some wild mine shafts and a few rotting—"

"You're a prince for easing my mind," she snapped.

"You're welcome." He smirked. "Well, I see my work here is done, so I'll go."

"*Must* you?"

Ignoring her gibe, he squeezed the boy's arm. "See you after breakfast, sport."

When he was gone, Lorna scanned the messy kitchen. She'd had no idea her day would start this early. "Honey, I'd really better go. Could you—? Would you mind—?"

He nodded. "I'll clean up." The sweet kid looked very much like his father at the moment. Those resolute green eyes, that stubborn chin. "See. I'm not a baby. I can do stuff!"

She hugged his thin shoulders. "You're my hero." Kissing him on the cheek, she grabbed her toolbox and headed for the door. "And after you're finished here, go straight to the hangar. Don't wander—"

"Mom!"

She shook her head at herself and hurried out the door for her first day as the official plumber of Brazen Gulch. On her way to the truck, she saw a curvy brunette walking toward the redbrick building, clinging to Clint's arm.

"Lord," she moaned, eyeing heaven. "If Sam *has* to go into his office, please don't let him forget to knock."

Clint saw Lorna out of the corner of his eye as he held the door for his newest flying student. She was hopping up into the cab of her absurd plumbing truck, wearing her cornflower-blue overalls with Willow Plumbing embroidered across the bib in the same script and rosy hue that was emblazoned on each door of her fire truck.

The engine chugged to life, and he pursed his lips, watching her serious face as she shifted into reverse. The woman was a strange and wondrous little bird. A frightened, brave thing who'd been deeply hurt. He liked her, but it was obvious she didn't trust him. Of course, that didn't make her *wrong.* He liked women—on a surface level. He enjoyed them for the pleasure and diversion they could give. Maybe not quite on the assembly-line basis the skeptical Mrs. Willow seemed to think. But he was rarely starved for companionship.

He did make it a rule never to get to know any one woman very well, however. He'd watched what had happened to his father because he allowed a woman emotional control over his dreams. That wouldn't happen to him.

So why did he have an urge to get to know this woman? Why did he want to figure out what made her so soft-hearted, yet so standoffish? He even wondered what had made her become a plumber, of all things? He sensed it had been because somebody else *needed* her to become a plumber.

"Hey, Clint?"

He blinked, startled to discover that he was still holding his door ajar, staring after a retreating fire truck painted a prissy blue.

"Coming, sweetheart." He grinned at his companion, wondering at himself for dwelling on a woman who made a fashion statement out of small mammals.

By lunchtime, Lorna was only a third of the way through her list of phone calls. She didn't have time to eat, but she was starving. The red neon sign of Orville's Diner beckoned as she approached along Brazen Gulch's main street, and she stared longingly at it from the cab of her truck. Her stomach growled. Darn that Clint McCord, showing up just when she'd been about to eat her breakfast. She couldn't go on fending off amorous customers if she didn't have the strength. A chicken sandwich or a bowl of stew would certainly help.

At one house, she'd been afraid to lie on her back under the sink for fear she would have to clunk the home-owner on the head with her pipe wrench and cry, "Rape!" She'd finally figured out a way to deal with him, by keeping him running up to the second floor as she shouted, "Is rusty water flooding out of the sink? Is the toilet over-flowing with sewage?"

She'd known it couldn't possibly happen, considering his minor plumbing problem. But the guy—Roger Garlic-Cures-Everything Wedmonger—didn't know any more about plumbing than the garlic that dangled like swollen globs of Spanish moss all around his kitchen.

By the time he'd run up and down the stairs forty times to check on each possible catastrophe she'd described, he'd been too tired to do anything but hold his chest and wheeze, "What does a heart attack feel like?"

She shook her head at herself for being so deceitful, but she didn't feel too guilty. After all, Roger's kitchen sink now had a brand-new trap, and once he got his breath back he'd been perfectly healthy. Best of all, there had been no need to trouble the police. All in all, a pretty good morning.

Unable to help herself, she braked the truck before the diner. She had to eat something. Once inside, she was delighted with the interior. Plain, clean, with a decor right out of the fifties. There was a counter on one side, and booths next to windows covered with red-and-white-checked café curtains. In between was a row of six round tables. It couldn't have seemed more like Mayberry's Bluebell Diner if Andy Taylor and Helen Crump had been snacking on apple pie in the corner booth.

The air was redolent with coffee, burgers and french fries, and the background noises consisted of sizzling food, clinking silverware and the low drone of noontime conversations.

The talking noises dimmed when she entered, and the mostly male clientele stared at her as though she'd just arrived from another planet. It must have been an appealing planet, however, for they were nudging each other and grinning. This was another example of how famished the town was for female companionship, for Lorna knew that, in her smudged overalls and waterproof boots, she was no Sharon Stone—Oliver Stone, maybe.

"Mom!"

She scanned the room. Nobody in the world said "Mom" quite like Sam. A skinny little arm popped up, fingers wagging. In the back, at the last table, she could see him. Her stomach clenched when she saw who he was with. There was Clint—*drat that grin*—McCord sitting across from him, along with two strange women. Why was she not surprised?

Wondering what sort of activities Mr. McCord was introducing her son to while she was at work, she changed directions and headed for them. Trying to maintain a calm facade, she scanned the table. "What's this, a double date?"

Clint stood, which nearly startled her out of her overalls. He dragged over an empty chair and patted its metal back. "Join us?"

She hesitated, glancing at Sam and trying to think of a reasonable excuse for collecting her son and escaping. But she was starving, and she decided she had to stay long enough to eat. "Well...wouldn't it be less crowded if Sam and I moved to another table?"

Clint shook his head, his expression indicating that her idea was not only bad, but unkind. "That would be cruel to Mavis."

Lorna felt thwarted, and didn't know why. She looked first at the buxom woman on Clint's right, who was wearing nurse's garb. Her hair was short, straight and black, and her lips were full and red. She was smiling; her little hazel eyes seemed friendly, if a bit crafty. The woman on Clint's left was tall and thin, with a round face and smallish features. Her hair was wispy, white-blond, giving her head the look of a dandelion bent on scattering its seed.

She wasn't beautiful, but pleasant-looking. Her smile was more tentative, almost nonexistent.

Lorna wondered which of Clint's female companions was Mavis, and why taking Sam away would be cruel to her. "I don't mean to upset you, Mavis." She addressed both women. "But when I left for work, maybe I should have told Mr. McCord I didn't feel my son was old enough to date."

"Aw, Mom," Sam objected. "Me and Clint just met these ladies. They're like you." With a droopy pickle slice, he indicated the buxom woman. "That's Reva Rosenblatt, who answered the ad for a nurse and—" He shifted, flipping the pickle in the thin woman's direction. "And that's—"

Before he could go on, Lorna removed the limp gherkin from his fingers and placed it on his plate, beside a half-eaten hamburger. "When I told you the rule about not pointing, I guess I should have mentioned not even with pickles."

"Oh, yeah—anyway, that's Thelma Boyle, the new librarian."

Lorna reached out and shook hands with the women, but remained confused. "Then who's Mavis?"

"She's our waitress," Clint said. "And she gets emotional if you make her do any more math than necessary. I'd suggest you join us. Watching Mavis do subtraction is not a pretty sight." He once again indicated the chair. "Besides, you three women have a lot in common."

That was true. She'd love to get to know a few of the town's women, for a change. Without further argument, she took the seat, wondering how Clint had managed to squeeze her chair in between his and Reva's. When seated, she had a hard time avoiding his thigh, but managed.

"Hi, y'all!" came a strident voice, the salutation punctuated by popping gum. When Lorna glanced around, she was sure she was face-to-face with the math-impaired Mavis. "What can I do ya for, honey?" She batted away a friendly pinch on the fanny from an admirer at a nearby booth. "Quit, Louie!" she told him with a wiggle of her tight yellow uniform. "If you want more coffee, there's a way to get my attention without bruisin' the merchandise." She grinned at Lorna, tossing short hair bleached so orange it looked like shredded cheddar cheese. "Wanna hear the specials?" she asked through loud gum-popping.

"Can I have a chicken sandwich?" she asked. "And coffee?"

"Sure, honey. Everything on that chick san?"

Clint nudged her leg. "Hold the onions."

She frowned at him, with an expression that suggested he would *never* get close enough to be offended by her onions. "Sure, everything," she told Mavis loudly. "Why not?"

"I tried," he murmured, sounding vaguely amused.

She pointedly shifted away from his touch.

"Want anything in the coffee, honey?"

She shook her head, turning her attention to her son as he gobbled up the rest of his burger. "How'd the morning go, Sam?"

He lifted his gaze, but his mouth was too full to respond.

"Sam was a big help, so I'm buying him lunch."

"Yeah—" The boy swallowed with effort. "I swept up, and—"

"He's so cute," Reva broke in, her big red lips splitting in an affectionate smile. "I hope someday I have ten just like him." Though she patted Sam's hand, her eyes kept shifting to Clint. It was clear the boy had been an excuse to get to the man.

Lorna couldn't blame Reva. From what she'd discovered so far, Clint was the best-looking man in town, with those midnight eyes and that hair that fell in such calculated dishevelment across his brow. If she hadn't already learned her lesson about wild, exciting men, even *she* might have been tempted. Shoving the notion away, she decided to take Reva's compliment to her son at face value, and smiled with pride. "You'll be lucky if you have even one little boy like Sam." She winked at him, and he grinned shyly.

"Well, I figure this is the place to get started," Reva whispered across the table. "I mean, all the *m-e-n*." She spelled the word, as though it were racy, then glanced stealthily at the boy, clearly pleased with herself that she'd spared him the naughty truth. Unfortunately, he wasn't two years old, and he could understand the word *men*, even spelled out in an overloud whisper.

"There seem to be a lot of nice people here," Lorna said, trying to change the subject.

"Say, Sam." Clint stood, shoving a hand into his pocket. "They've got a great video game around by the jukebox. If you're through, be my guest. Mavis can change these for you."

Sam hopped up, but looked at his mother for permission to take the dollar bills. Though she didn't really want him accepting Clint's money, she decided it was better than having him sit here and listen to Reva spell. She nodded. "Sure." As Sam ran off, she turned to Clint. "In exchange for the video money, I'll snake your pipes."

He chuckled. "Mrs. Willow, you make me blush."

She eyed heaven. "Will you *quit!*"

"You brought it up," he teased with a shrug.

Her coffee came, giving her a few seconds to count to ten, but she couldn't help asking, "How does it happen that with a diner full of men, you end up with *all* the women?"

He took a bite of his taco, then said, "Only the new ones."

"Okay—the *new* ones."

"Oh, Sam was just so darling, I asked if I could join them," Reva said. "And Thelma was with me. Right, Thel?"

The thin woman nodded, her glance lowered to her bowl of vegetable soup.

"Where are the rest of the women who are supposed to be crawling all over town?" Lorna wondered aloud.

"Should be up and around anytime." Reva fished around in her bag and came up with a lipstick. "They're here to party, party, party. Not like us working stiffs who have to get up at the crack of dawn. From what I hear, the backhoe company's having a lot of guys calling in sick these days." Lorna was fascinated by how the woman managed to apply her lipstick and talk at the same time. "Oh, well, once all the party gals leave, *we'll* still be here, won't we, Thel?"

The other woman dabbed at her mouth with her paper napkin, nodding. Her cheeks were crimson spots of embarrassment at being singled out to make a comment.

"Thel's shy," Reva said, replacing her lipstick in her bag. "But she already has dates for every night this week, don't you, Thel?"

The quiet woman nodded again, her face fairly glowing from the unwanted attention. "Thel and I are sharing a room in Mrs. Crooner's rooming house. We came here together from Brownsville last week. What about you?"

She finished a sip of coffee. "Sam and I are from Dal—"

"I know that part from Clint and Sam. And about the lightning fire. I meant, how's your date book shaping up?"

Reva grinned wickedly, and Lorna had an uneasy feeling she was about to spell something, so she jumped in. "Uh, I'm going to be busy most evenings, yes." She heaved a weary sigh, and was startled to hear it. She'd had no idea how unexcited she was about her first crop of dates.

"Something wrong with that?" Reva looked stunned at the very idea that a week full of dates wasn't seven days in heaven.

Lorna laughed at herself, feeling ridiculous. "Nothing's wrong. It's just that I'd like to meet one guy in this town who doesn't say, 'If I show you my plumbing, you have to show me yours.'"

Even through Reva's guffaw, Lorna could hear Clint clear his throat, and she glowered at him. "Is every guy in town a member of some secret society for the preservation of stupid sexual innuendos?"

"If I told you that, it wouldn't be a secret." His smile was decidedly masculine, and she felt a trickle of longing. He was a gorgeous specimen, sitting there, with those broad shoulders and dark, laughing eyes. Her glance trailed across the triangle of chest hair curling in the unbuttoned V of his shirt. She could hardly tear her gaze away, but forced herself. Troubled that every inch of the man seemed to warm her blood, she muttered, "I'm surprised *you* haven't used that awful plumbing line, too."

"It must be the Sir Walter Raleigh in me."

She refused to look at him and made sure her thigh wasn't brushing his, but he was close enough that she could register his body heat, and she felt uncomfortably warm. She hoped she was coming down with the flu.

Her chicken sandwich clanked down in front of her, and she made herself focus on the safe, mundane subject of her lunch. Taking a big bite, she chewed. After a few seconds, she noticed burning in her mouth and on her tongue, and her eyes teared up. Grabbing her water, she downed it, trying to quench the fire. It was like emptying an eyedropper into a volcano. She gagged and choked, wondering when smoke would start pouring from her lips.

"Orville grows his own onions." Clint handed her his glass, which she snatched and gulped down while praying to die. "Something about the soil around his place makes them as hot as jalapeños." He leaned her way. "My suggestion about holding the onions was strictly landlord-to-tenant, Mrs. Willow. Kissing you was the farthest thing from my mind." Impertinent laughter lit his eyes. "Well, almost the farthest thing."

3

It had been a mistake to make a date for her first working night in town. Irritated with herself, Lorna looked at her watch. The last thing she wanted to do tonight was go out to dinner with a complete stranger. Lunch with Clint and company had been traumatic enough. Well, maybe Joe wasn't a complete stranger. She knew he was a foreman at the Brazen Backhoe plant and that his toilet had a brand-new ball-cock assembly.

She'd had a terrible time this morning explaining to Joe what was wrong with his toilet. Somehow telling a man he needed a new ball cock had never gotten easy for her, even after eight years as a plumber. Upon getting that news, men either paled and stuttered or leered and said, "Wanna try me, sweetie?"

She finished drying her hands and hung the towel on the bathroom rack. Joe had been in the category of men who paled, poor dear, and *that* was the reason she'd accepted the date with him. The less cocky a man acted around her, the more chance he had of winning her heart—someday...maybe....

Hearing a knock at the living room door, she called out, "Sam, honey, get that for me, please. It's probably Joe and his sister."

"His what?" he shouted from the living room.

"His little sister, Janet. Your sitter for tonight."

Sam's grumble told her he wasn't happy about that, but it couldn't be helped. Not for a few years, at least. She gave herself one last, critical glance in the bathroom mirror. Her hair had always been naturally curly, but with today's corkscrew styles, people usually assumed she had a brand-new permanent. She nervously fluffed the shoulder-length curls, which was about all the control she had over the stuff.

A dark blond clump fell across one eye, and she swept it back. "Okay, Joe," she murmured aloud. "I'm as ready as I'll ever be."

The night was muggy, so she'd decided to wear an embroidered denim vest as her blouse. She'd gotten it on sale, and it went perfectly with a blue-and-pink print broomstick skirt she'd made. Padding barefoot to the tiny bedroom closet, she grabbed a pair of strappy navy sandals and slipped them on. One immediately fell off. Confused, she examined it, only to find that every single one of the five straps that went across the arch had been chewed through. *"Barney!"* she muttered under her breath. "You chew up *one* more pair of shoes, Buster, and you really will be a hat!" Deciding she had little choice, she grabbed her lug-soled boots and a pair of pink socks and hurriedly put them on.

When she emerged from the bedroom, she was surprised to see Clint, not Joe and his sister, lounging on the sofa. He had a hedgehog in his lap and a squirrel in his hair. "Hi." He grinned, as though he spent many happy hours looking like an L. L. Bean Christmas tree. "Sam tells me that since I'm still conscious, Barney thinks I'm not a dork."

"I'm delighted a squirrel's opinion makes you so cheerful." She glanced away from his smile, forcing herself to remember what had happened the last time she felt so foolish about a man.

Sam was standing in the entry to the kitchen. "Hi, Mom." He held an unopened package of cookies. "Clint's out of eggs."

She eyed the cellophane container in his hands. "I hate to break it to you, kiddo, but I've quit keeping the eggs in the Oreo bag."

He grinned impishly. "I kinda thought your date might like one."

She gave him a stern look. "Don't you *dare*, young man."

"That's not very hospitable," Clint said. "I've heard Joe loves Oreos. So do I, for that matter."

"So does Barney." Lorna plunked her hands on her hips. "Show Mr. McCord how much Barney loves cookies, Sam."

The boy made his "No fair" face, then took an Oreo from the package. In a flash, Barney was airborne, leaping from Clint's head to the coffee table then bounding to the armchair and lunging off at a right angle to fling himself at Sam. He landed on the boy's skinny arm, scampered to his hand, grabbed the cookie and dangled from it, eating away.

"Whoa!" Clint chuckled. "Great trick."

"And it's scared off more than one of my dates. They tend to run away, screaming, 'Rat!'" She continued to eye her son and his furry parasite. "Samuel, I will not have you frightening people like that. You could give somebody a heart attack."

"Barney doesn't look like a rat," Sam protested. The squirrel dropped to the floor with the rest of the cookie clutched in his jaws and scampered behind the couch. "Does he look like a rat, Clint?"

The man grinned and winked at Sam. "Anybody who can't tell a squirrel from a rat deserves what he gets." Scooping up Aunt Bee, he settled her inside her cage, then stood.

"You're a huge help," she muttered. The room was small, and she didn't care to be within touching distance of Clint, so she backed away, but came up short against the cabin door.

His shrug was easy and nonchalant. Clearly, he wasn't having any problems with their close proximity. "Happy to help, ma'am."

"I'll get your eggs." Sam spun toward the kitchen.

"Have you eaten, sport?" Clint asked.

"Yeah. Mom made me some spinach meat loaf."

Clint's laugh was rich and deep. "No. Seriously."

"What's wrong with spinach meat loaf?" Lorna asked, affronted.

When he reached the entrance to the kitchen, he faced her and leaned against the wall. "For one thing, it's a combination of the two most disgusting foods in the civilized world."

"See, Mom!" Sam came up beside Clint and handed him the eggs. "That's what I keep saying."

She glared at the two males in the kitchen entryway. "My father taught me to cook."

"Who taught him, the Marquis de Sade?"

"That's lovely, Mr. McCord. Borrow my eggs, then insult my family." There was a knock at the door, and she spun to fling it wide. *"What?"*

Joe's mustache drooped, a sure sign his smile had faded, and the hand that held a bouquet of daisies fell to his side. "Uh..."

She closed her eyes, upset with herself that she'd completely forgotten about him. Working on a smile, she pulled the door wide. "Oh, hi, Joe." She took his hand and tugged him inside. "Mr. McCord and Sam and I were just, er, playing a game." She couldn't think of a way to make that feeble lie work, so she shut her mouth and hoped he wouldn't demand details. Luckily, he merely handed her the daisies.

As Lorna closed the door, Clint held up the eggs for Joe to see. "I won," he joked.

Lorna had a sudden thought and looked back outside. "Where's your sister, Joe?"

"Oh, uh, that . . ." He sounded sheepish. "Didn't Janet call you?"

She frowned at her date, then swung to look at Clint. "Did I get any calls?"

He shook his head. "Nope."

She looked at Joe. "Isn't she coming?"

He scratched his neck, then adjusted his collar nervously. "She might be late." He shrugged. "Told me she'd call and explain."

He nodded a greeting to Clint, looking uncomfortable in his ill-fitting suit. Clint nodded back.

Lorna took Joe's arm to get his attention. "How late will she be?"

He looked upset. "Thirty minutes . . . maybe?"

That was all she needed! Exasperated, she shook her head. "I can't just go off and leave my son alone."

"I'll be fine for a half hour, Mom," Sam lamented. "Besides, Clint's close by."

Joe looked miserable, but no more miserable than she felt.

"Sam can come over and eat with me. I'm cooking spaghetti," Clint offered.

"What about your date?" Lorna asked.

He shrugged. "That's later. It'll work out fine."

"*Please,* Mom?" Sam whined.

"Janet's very reliable," Joe interjected, doing a little whining of his own.

She exhaled, glancing from Joe-of-the-wrinkled-brow to Clint to Sam, who was so animated by the idea of having Clint's spaghetti, it made her want to scream. She had an urge to cancel the whole evening, but decided it was an overreaction. Janet would be there shortly. Clint's date wouldn't be disrupted, and Sam would eat again—something that couldn't hurt his toothpick frame. "Well . . . okay," she said with heavy reluctance.

Sam squealed with delight. Clint grinned and slung an arm around the boy's shoulders. "Don't worry, Mom," he teased. "I'll hide the knives and cover the electric sockets. He'll be fine."

She slanted a scowl at him, but couldn't mean it. "Thanks," she finally murmured, exhibiting a grateful smile.

She noticed the eggs in his hand, and her frown returned as she indicated them with a nod. "What are those for, if you're making spaghetti?"

A well-formed eyebrow rose. "Breakfast."

The merriment in his gaze was galling, and she stiffened. *Breakfast! Naturally, his late date was staying for breakfast.* She *had* to ask!

He strolled toward the door, his arm still around Sam's shoulders, then stopped beside Joe. "Hey, man, which would you say is worse, a rat eating a cookie out of your hand, or *you* eating spinach meat loaf?"

Joe's beefy face screwed up, and he scratched his balding head. "Shucks! That's a hard choice."

Clint placed the eggs in Joe's hands. "We have a winner and new champion." Cocking a kidding brow in Lorna's direction, he steered her son out the door.

* * *

Clint was restless and bored. He knew Lorna had thought he had a date, and it had amused him to let her think it at the time. But he didn't. Hadn't felt like it. Now, though, he was regretting his decision. He'd been pleasantly surprised when his mechanic, Bo Pickett, arrived back early. Together, Clint, Sam and Bo had fixed spaghetti and a big salad, while Bo talked about his two sons, looking melancholy. Divorce was hell.

Dinner had been pleasant, and Bo's mood had brightened with Sam around. After the three males did the dishes, Bo had taken his bags upstairs and unpacked while Sam and Clint played video games. Interestingly, the "reliable" Janet had never shown up at all.

Around nine, Sam had fallen asleep watching a "MacGyver" rerun, and restlessness had overtaken Clint again. When Bo assured him that he'd look after the boy, Clint had headed into town.

Now he lounged at a table in Orville's Diner, surrounded by visiting women. As he entered, they'd swooped down on him like crows after the last ear of corn. He had quickly lost interest in their flirting and fawning, and was hardly listening. His eyes were on one particular waitress buzzing from table to table, serving coffee and taking orders. The reason he was so taken with her was that he happened to know she'd never been in the diner before noon today, when she'd almost died from onion poisoning.

Also, at noon today she'd been a plumber.

Tonight, this same waitress had had a date. He knew that, too, because he'd been with her when her date came to pick her up. She was still on that date, it seemed, since Joe was sitting in one of the booths—all alone and looking ticked off. Clint was a little ticked, too, wondering if

Joe had any inkling that his sister had never had any intention of doing any baby-sitting.

Lorna skimmed by Clint's table, and he put a detaining hand on her wrist. "The plumbing business in a slump, Mrs. Willow?"

"Oh—hi..." She clearly hadn't noticed that he'd come into the crowded diner, because her expression went from a serving-wench smile to a self-conscious frown. "What are you doing here? I thought you had a date."

He ran a hand through his hair, feeling a sudden urge to see those honey-brown eyes sparking at him. "She was so taken with Sam, she rejected me for him. I left the two young lovers at my place."

He was rewarded by her alarmed expression. It was weird how the passion in those big, expressive eyes made him feel alive. It was almost like the exhilaration he felt when he was soaring above the clouds in his plane.

"That's not funny, Mr. McCord."

He shrugged. "Okay. Truth? I didn't have a date. My mechanic got back early, so he and Sam helped me eat the spaghetti. By the time I left, your son was safe and asleep." Deciding not to burden her with the news about the absent Janet, he indicated the coffeepot sloshing in her hand. "Now, answer my question. What's with the new career?"

She exhaled, swiping curls from her eyes. "Mavis was upset."

He indicated her gloomy date with a nod. "It seems to be going around."

Lorna's gaze followed his to Joe's booth, and she bit her lower lip. "Oh, dear..."

"What was the crisis that did Mavis in? Did somebody make her do subtraction?"

She turned back, adding coffee to one of his female companions' cups without paying much attention to what she was doing. "Hmmm? Oh—Mavis? Poor thing caught one of her steady boyfriends with someone else."

"That shouldn't be new for her."

Lorna looked unbelieving. "How can you be so insensitive? She was *crying*. I had to do something."

He glanced at Joe. "I think Joe's going to start crying in a minute."

She peered guiltily at her abandoned date. "Oh, no. Why do these things always happen to me?"

He took a sip of his coffee. "They don't if you don't let them."

She jerked around and gave him a tight-lipped smile. "Will there be anything else, *sir?*" Before he could answer, she marched off in a huff.

He watched her go to Joe and pour him some coffee. By her body language and her expression, it was clear she was trying to apologize for her capriciousness. Joe continued to frown, even in the face of her animated repentance. *Jerk.* Clint had a feeling any man who fell for Lorna—the softhearted will-o'-the-wisp—would have to be like a reed in the mercurial wind of her personality. Not a bad fate, he decided, for somebody who *wanted* roots.

He turned his attention to the women who'd joined him at his table—Gerrymander, Weather Vane, Taffeta and Monotony—something like that. To be honest, their names didn't matter to him. Women were passing pleasures in his life. Flying was his real passion. He'd decided long ago he didn't want strings. Wouldn't allow disapproval. He was his own master, and planned to keep it that way.

When one of the women—Monolith or Molecule or whatever—pouted prettily that the jukebox was no longer playing, he took the opportunity to stretch his legs and went to plug in a few quarters.

While he was glancing through the tunes, Lorna came by carrying a tray of dirty dishes, whispering, "I thought you said you weren't interested in finding a wife."

"That's true." He didn't look at her, but continued to peruse the tune list, though after a year in town he knew them by heart. "But I figure, since women love to tame men, I'll let them practice on me."

"Really?" she asked archly. "So how many have tamed *you* this week?"

"Why?" He pushed a random button, with no idea what melody he'd chosen. "Would you like a little practice, too?" He peered her way.

She harrumphed, looking disdainful and vaguely unsettled by his invitation. "I—I don't want to tame any man. That's a snare and a delusion. I want one who's already tame."

He bent toward her in a confiding gesture. "Well, good luck with Mr. Tame number two, because number one looks like he's tired of waiting."

She whirled around and moaned as Joe stalked through the diner and headed out the door without a backward glance. "Oh, no. I promised him it wouldn't be much longer."

"How is it he didn't take you to the hotel dining room for dinner? This isn't a very classy joint for a date."

"Oh…" She shifted her tray, sounding morose. "Since there are so many women in town, they've had to start taking reservations over there, and Joe forgot. So we ended up here."

"He'll remember next time. People learn from their mistakes."

He was rewarded with one of her big-eyed, astounded glances. "Don't tell me you think he'd ask me out *again?*"

He shrugged, lounging against the jukebox. "Do you care?"

She frowned, as though thinking about that for the first time. "Actually... I guess not."

He didn't know why that made him feel like smiling, but he did. "See. You learned something tonight, and you'll go home with a purse full of tips. Not a bad evening."

Her lips lifted ever so slightly, and he could tell she wasn't delighted to find him in any way wise or helpful. Her vague smile disappeared. "You don't take much seriously, do you?"

"Not much." He pushed away from the jukebox, his impulse to grin fading, too. "When your shift is over, let me know. I'll give you a ride home."

He watched her as she scanned his table. When she faced him again, her expression was mistrustful. "Isn't six a crowd?"

For some reason, he wanted to take her into his arms, to kiss the wariness from her eyes and replace it with sweet surrender. It frustrated the fire out of him that she wanted nothing to do with him. How could one unwilling woman, among so many eager ones, prick his ego that way?

Deciding he was an idiot to stew over it, he leaned toward her, as though to share a secret. "Don't panic, Mrs. Willow. I *think* I can control myself from having group sex long enough to give you a ride home."

As he ambled away, he wondered again why she thought he was such a sex maniac. To be honest, he hadn't been with a woman in—well, long enough. It hadn't given him much of a rush lately. He glanced back at Lorna as she zipped through the kitchen door to deposit her dishes. Inhaling, he shrugged his hands into his pockets. He had a feeling little Miss Plumber would give him quite a rush. What a shame she'd insist that hell freeze over first.

Lorna hugged the door handle of Clint's open-air Jeep as he drove her home. Yet, even as uneasy as she was, she found herself enjoying the feel of the wind in her hair, the dry-pine scent of sagebrush and the cool night air on her face.

What she didn't enjoy was the way the moonlight combined with the night shadows to stage Clint's features in a stark tableau of masculine perfection. She'd never noticed how sculpted his features were—as though carved from granite by a daring, imaginative artist. In this light, he didn't look easygoing at all, but iron-willed, even hawkish. When his eyebrows dipped, as they did now, he reminded her of a bird of prey.

She balled her hands in her lap. The last thing she wanted was to be the mouse he set his sights on for tonight's tumble in the grass. Casual sex was *not* what she'd come to Brazen Gulch to find. But when she left Orville's Diner that evening, she'd only been able to look on in horror as Clint gently deflected his companions' come-ons and ended up taking her home—alone!

She breathed deeply, evenly, trying to control her heart rate. She was so afraid that if he aimed those seductive eyes her way she might not have the desire to run from him.

Right now, he was strangely serious and quiet. She wondered what was on his mind, but thought better of asking. Maybe it was good that his mind was somewhere else. She'd be smart not to remind him that she was in the car at all. It would be best if she sat still and kept quiet. Once they got to the airfield, she could leap out and yell her thanks on the run.

It might be chickenhearted, but sometimes the cowardly way was the smartest way out of a situation. She didn't know if anybody had ever said that, but if not, they should have. She vowed that if she made it out of this situation without...without...well, she planned to have her praise for cowardliness embroidered on a pillow.

When Clint drove onto the asphalt parking lot and pulled alongside her truck, she was out of the Jeep and ten feet away before he called, "Goodnight, Mrs. Willow."

She waved, dashed away and mumbled something about appreciating the ride and needing to get up early.

"And don't worry about Sam. I'll give him some breakfast."

She faltered and twirled to face him. *"What?"*

Why would Sam be at his place? Her heart hammered as she watched her clean-escape scenario dissolve before her eyes. What had he done—seduce the naive Janet, then held her own son hostage in exchange for sex with her, too?

Clint got out of the Jeep and headed toward her. "I said, I'd—"

"For what earthly reason is he at your house?"

He looked at her curiously, as though her accusatory tone were an overreaction. *Yeah! Sure! He was good. Real good! He'd known what he was doing when he invited Sam into his web, er, house!*

"To be honest, there was a little something I didn't tell you."

Now the truth was coming out! *The sex maniac!* Brushing curls from her eyes, she demanded, "What have you done? Janet was only seventeen, you know!"

"No, I wouldn't know. She never showed." He shrugged. "Sam and Bo ate spaghetti with me. Later we did some TV. Kind of a summer-rerun ménage à trois. It's ugly, but I'm glad it's finally out in the open."

"Janet never came?" she breathed, in shock.

"Nope." He canted his head, his boyish charm sabotaging her resolve. Okay, so maybe he'd come to her rescue. Maybe he'd simply fed Sam spaghetti and let him watch TV until he fell asleep. There was a *slim* possibility that it hadn't been a sinister plot to get her naked, after all. "Am I supposed to believe you *like* kids?" she asked, still wary of his motives.

He gave her a smirk that spelled trouble, and she swallowed. "Okay, copper." He stalked toward her like a cocky B-movie punk. "Ain't you supposed to read me my rights?"

He was very near now. She wanted to be flippant right back, but her brain was getting foggy. The only thing she was absolutely sure of was how nice his after-shave smelled in the moonlight. If he'd invited Sam over to his place with the idea of seducing her, then it had been a brilliant stroke. She had half a mind to leap into his arms and let nature take its course.

"You're supposed to tell me I have the right to remain silent," he said softly.

She blinked, staring into those black satin eyes. Their message was paralyzing. "Hmmm?"

"And I have the right to counsel." Somehow, his lips seemed nearer—or did they?

"Anything I say can be used against me...."

Her heart hammered in helpless denial. This couldn't be happening. He was seducing her, and he wasn't saying anything seductive. Good grief, if what he was quoting was sexy, all the cops on the beat would have every felon planting big wet kisses right on their mouths.

Shouldn't he be saying, "You're beautiful" or "You have a great tush"? Something she could hang her hat on as a seduction, and use as an excuse to slap him silly? The man was even better than she'd feared. He was reading himself his rights, for heaven's sake, and she was teetering toward him as though he were a magnet and she were a very stupid paper clip.

"You don't want to do this, do you?"

He asked the question almost too quietly for her to hear, and she faltered in midteeter. "I— What?"

His grin was rueful. "You *really* don't want to have sex with me, do you?"

He'd moved a hair's breadth away, not far enough to release her completely from his spell, but far enough to allow a little sanity to return. Unable to get words past her paralyzed throat, she could only shake her head.

"Why?"

He asked the question without rancor, but there was an edge of frustration in the word that he wasn't able to hide. She bit her lip. "Because . . . because . . ."

"Because I'm not interested in marriage?"

That was a good reason. But it was *his* reason, not hers. "I wouldn't marry you even if you were interested," she whispered.

He looked startled, as though he didn't hear that very often. "Don't be bashful, Mrs. Willow. I can take the truth." He grinned that smart-aleck grin, and her heart missed a beat. "Okay. I won't press it." He touched her hand, and squeezed. His fingers lingered for several seconds, warm and solid, and then he dropped her hand. "If you change your mind, let me know."

She shook her head in consternation. "You're amazingly resilient."

He chuckled, but there was a tinge of melancholy in it. "I'll bring Sam over after breakfast."

She turned to go, but felt a halting hand on her wrist. "Just one more thing." She looked back, and before she could guess what was happening, he was kissing her, and doing a wonderful job. The caress of his lips was easy, practiced, but so wildly thrilling she couldn't conjure up any anger for his intimate trespass.

His mouth moved lazily, sensuously, and with such bold sureness she wanted to scream. Or did she want to cry out with desire because of the way his tongue licked and teased, tempting her to give in, to open herself to his sweet exploration?

She clung to him, fighting her attraction and losing. She hated her weakness for this inappropriate man. But his appeal was undeniable. Even the pulsing promise of his heartbeat made her insides melt and meld into one white-hot mass of longing. She'd known this feeling only once in her life before, and she'd promised herself never to let it sway her again. Clint was exactly the wrong man for her.

Though she berated herself, she opened her lips with a crazy, urgent need to feel his questing tongue pleasure the deepest recesses of her mouth.

He groaned against her lips, drawing her more fully against his hard body. His arousal made her quiver, and she arched against him, thirsting for more. *Where was sanity when you needed it?* She was lost again, *lost....*

He lifted his lips slightly, murmuring, "Liar." The husky word sounded like an endearment. How ironic. He hadn't said anything loving or tender, but she wanted to claw his clothes from him and ravish him, maybe even howl at the moon when it was done.

Though she struggled to deny his taunting admonition, she could only cling to him wantonly, loathing herself. "You're good...." she cried weakly. "I hate you for that."

His kissed her jaw. "You don't hate me."

"I—do." Her voice broke, and it was only then she realized she was crying.

His lips hesitated in their delicious quest, and Lorna could tell he'd detected her desolation. "Hell," he whispered, lifting his head. Watchful eyes searched her face. *"Damn."* Reluctantly, he let her go. "I didn't mean to..." He shook his head, clearly angry with himself. "Damn, I'm sorry...."

She was so humiliated she couldn't speak, could barely stand.

For another moment, he stood there, tall, gorgeous and furious with himself. Then he half grinned. It wasn't an expression of humor, but one of apology. "That wasn't very landlordlike, was it?"

She shook her head. "Not—not very."

He exhaled long and low, as though trying to regain his composure. "Damn," he said again, turning away. "Good night, Mrs.—"

"It's not that I don't find you attractive," she broke in, wishing she didn't have to say this, but knowing that for some reason she did.

He shifted back. Even frowning, he had a sexual charisma that tugged at her heart, made her words weak and thready. "It...it's just that Bill—Sam's father—was like you. Wild. He was even nicknamed Wild Bill. A race-car driver." Her gaze fell to her feet. "I learned the hard way not to get involved with excitement junkies."

There was a long silence, when all she could hear was a distant, bony rattle of sagebrush bouncing along the asphalt runway.

"If you want boring sex—I could try."

There was that nonchalant tone again. How dare he be so casual, when she was pouring out her deepest feelings! Her gaze rocketed to meet his. "Don't put yourself out!"

"No trouble." The set of his shoulders was a dismissal. What had happened? What had suddenly made him so indifferent to her? Trying to ignore the stab of pain that shot through her chest, she warned, "I have two rules I live by, Mr. McCord. First, I'm not into casual sex, and second, I don't date men with a death wish."

He lifted his head in a half nod. "Thanks for sharing."

She hugged herself, suddenly cold. "Well—under the circumstances, maybe I'd better get Sam."

"Under what circumstances?"

She rubbed her arms, squirming under his narrowed gaze. "You know what circumstances."

"You mean the you-won't-have-sex-with-me-so-your-son-can't-sleep-under-my-roof circumstances?"

She felt defeated. "You don't have to make it sound silly."

"It is silly."

She looked away, moving restlessly. "Okay. I'm too tired to argue. Have it your way." Spinning on her heel, she fled.

"You're welcome, Mrs. Willow."

Her jaw tightened as she headed toward her cottage. Damn him for making her feel like the delinquent here.

4

The next morning, Lorna couldn't force down her oatmeal. She kept hopping up, running to the window to watch for Sam. The last thing she wanted to do was go to Clint's place and ask for her son back. She fretted, stared at her bowl of congealing cereal and jumped up to look out the window again. She sighed and returned to her chair. Where was he? It was time for her to get to work. She couldn't just leave, not knowing if her son was okay.

Heaving another sigh, she picked up her bowl, scraping the gluey contents into the trash. "Don't let your pride get the better of you, Lorna. You have to collect your son, even if you're forced to face Clint to do it."

It was already warm at seven in the morning, and it was going to be a scorcher of a day. Absently she pulled her hair back in a stubby ponytail and secured it with the rubber band from the bread wrapper. Taking the last crusty piece from the plastic bag, she tossed it onto a plate, beside some raisins. "Okay, Barney," she muttered listlessly. "Chow down. Unless you're still too full of daisies."

The squirrel startled her by dropping from the light fixture above the table, right into the middle of the slice of bread. She stroked his soft back. "Your table manners could use a brushup, pal."

He ignored her, gobbling raisins. She turned toward the door, with reluctance. "Don't trouble yourself to worry, Barn, just because Sam might be chained in the attic by a couple of ax-wielding maniacs. I can handle it."

She didn't look back to see whether Barney was tearing into the bread or staring in horrified concern about Sam's situation. She had a feeling she knew which he was doing.

As the cottage door swung shut behind her, she plodded toward the redbrick building, wanting nothing more in the world than to see her son run out, ready to join her in the truck. But as hard as she wished it, Sam didn't magically appear. Bolstering her courage, she knocked on Clint's door. When it swung open, she was pleasantly surprised to see her son standing there, beaming.

"Morning, Mom!"

Her heart was so full of relief, she had a hard time looking stern. "Well, young man, I was beginning to think you'd run away to join the circus."

He looked puzzled. "Why would I do that?"

She smiled. Maybe that was too old a cliché for him to connect with. She touched his cheek. "Okay, you're right. Why leave the one we already have?"

"Hey, Clint!" he shouted into the bowels of the building. "It's Mom!"

She shook her head, shushing him. "Honey, we don't need to bother Mr. McCord. I just wanted to get you. It's time to go to work."

"But he fixed me breakfast. Don't you want to thank him?"

Lorna bit the inside of her cheek, managing to hide her flinch. "Oh—sure." Her tone wasn't convincing, but Sam didn't seem to notice.

Clint appeared suddenly, shirtless, his hair pleasantly tousled. "Hi," he said with a grin. "Hungry?"

She shook her head, trying to remain the cool, aloof tenant. "I—I really appreciate your feeding Sam. I'll repay you one of these days."

He put a hand on the boy's shoulder. "Not on fernburger night, I hope."

Sam made the international gag-me sign, sticking his finger in his mouth, then joined Clint in laughter. Lorna wasn't pleased about how close the two were becoming. It would only complicate things. "Come in and meet Bo." The boy waved her forward with his half-eaten piece of toast. "He's got a curly red beard he lets you hang on. And he can wiggle his ears one at a time!"

"It sounds tempting, but I've got to go to work, and I think we've imposed on Mr. McCord enough for one day." Why did she have to register Clint's half-naked slouch against the doorjamb so completely?

"It only takes a minute to hang on a man's beard," Clint said, laughter in his eyes.

She forced herself to look at him and his taunting grin. "I doubt if it would take me *that* long, but I really need to get going."

"But Mom," Sam objected. "Bo and Clint and me are gonna wash the Bearcat, then overhaul the crankpots."

Clint chuckled. "Close enough, sport." He squeezed the boy's shoulder, but continued to look at Lorna. His smile dimmed enough that she could tell he was serious. "Bo misses his boys. Sam's doing him a favor by being here."

She stared at Clint, at those captivating midnight eyes. She was learning the hard way that his gaze was very good at persuasion, seductive and otherwise, for she found herself nodding her consent. "Okay—if you're sure."

He winked at the boy. "See, sport? I told you she'd fall under my spell."

She stiffened, upset that she'd been manipulated. She had half a mind to take back her permission, but when his glance held hers again, his eyes were communicating something entirely different from what he'd said to Sam. Something about how that was all a lie, that she was anything but someone who easily fell for his charm.

She was startled to find that he'd been making a joke on himself—a private joke between the two of them. She found it interesting that he was secure enough within himself even to hint at last night. But then again, why not? The man didn't take anything seriously. He'd admitted that. Why would one rejection send him spiraling into a pit of self-doubt?

Sam squealed with delight and ran back into the house, leaving Clint and Lorna silently watching each other. After a second, he winked at her. "How's everything with you today, tenant?"

She took the hint. He wasn't going to hold what she'd said against her. They were going to get along as acquaintances. Period. She smiled, and for the first time it felt real. "Fine, landlord. And thanks about Sam."

"He's a great kid."

She nodded. "We can agree on that, at least." Then she had a thought. "Just—just don't take him up in a plane or do anything dangerous with him."

He lifted a skeptical eyebrow. "Damn. We were going to bungee-jump off the hangar later."

She realized he was being sarcastic, but she couldn't help the way she felt. She knew his type all too well. Bill had risked both her life and the life of their unborn child by racing along country roads at over a hundred miles an hour, ignoring her protests, insisting he wasn't doing anything foolish. She'd been scared to death half their married life, but too crazy in love to do anything about it. "I just want to make sure we understand each other."

His grin grew cynical as he shrugged away from the doorjamb. "Nope. You want to make sure I understand you."

When he closed the door, she remained there, staring, totally confused.

Lorna wasn't in the mood to go out with another of Brazen Gulch's bachelors. She'd fended off more than her share already today. To be fair, she supposed, that was the downside of getting the job here. But the upside was, she'd never had so much business in her life. If things went on like this, she could put money aside for Sam to attend college.

Pulling her truck into the flying school parking lot, she turned off the ignition and lay back against the cracked leather seat, feeling drained. She closed her eyes. Surely tonight would be better than the fiasco with Joe last evening. She told herself that this time, she would *not* take on anybody else's job, not pick up any strays, not fall victim to her soft heart in any way, shape or form. Clyde seemed like a great man. Funny, cute, kind. Maybe a little weird about the game of canasta, but otherwise normal.

She heard a rumbling that grew louder and louder, drawing her from her reverie. Opening her eyes, she saw the cause of the thundering sound through the windshield of her truck. A plane, high in the sky, was spiraling toward earth. She jerked forward to stare, her heart in her throat, as it tumbled out of control. "Oh, my Lord..." She slowly became aware that she was witnessing the crash of Clint's plane. "Oh...my...*Lord!*" She leaped from the cab and began to run toward the plunging plane, feeling helpless. There was nothing she could do. Nothing! All the same, stark horror and panic came rushing back to her, the same horror she'd felt on the day she watched Bill's car spin out of control and crash into the retaining wall, exploding into a ball of fire. Almost too weak to stand, she stumbled to a halt, covering her eyes. She couldn't bear to watch someone die such a ghastly death. Not again.

Seconds ticked by. Ponderous, cruel seconds. She felt sick. But the crash didn't come. She held her breath, squeezing tears back, but it still didn't come. Her heart thudding with fear, she took a tentative peek between her fingers. Nothing. She could see nothing.

But she could hear a faraway buzzing sound now. Removing her hands from her face, she scanned the sky. A flash caught her eye. Clint's plane was reflected in the sunlight as it went straight upward, through broken clouds. She inhaled deeply, fighting the nausea that had threatened to overcome her.

Still in a state of shock, she registered the fact that Sam was running toward her. He was naturally skinny, and his oversize T-shirt and shorts made him look as if he were constructed of wire. "Did you see that?" His face was alight with excitement.

"Yes— I . . ." Shaking her head, she tried to clear it. "Yes . . ."

"Killer, wasn't it?"

"Very." She breathed deeply while her heart rate dropped back toward normal.

"Come on." Sam grabbed her hand and began to tug her toward the runway. "He's coming in. I gotta tell him how great that was."

She didn't want to be dragged over there. "Honey, I have to get ready for a date."

He stopped pulling and turned. "Another dork?"

She frowned at him. "Young man. Is that any way to talk? You haven't even met Clyde."

He lifted a thin shoulder. "Okay. But don't you want to tell Clint he was killer?"

She shook her head. "I'm sure he knows how killer he is. And you need to take a shower while I get dinner. You look like you've been rolling in dirt."

"It's dusty out here."

"Well, not as dusty as it was before you got here. You have most of it on your hide."

The single-engine plane set down and whizzed along the runway, catching Lorna's attention. Clint was still some distance away, but she knew that as soon as he brought his plane to a stop, he'd be within shouting distance. Which was too close for her taste. She laid an arm about Sam's shoulders. "I'll fix us some dinner while you get cleaned up."

She didn't turn toward the airplane as Clint got out, but she knew exactly when he did, for Sam waved. "Gotta go eat dinner!" he shouted. "See you later!"

Clint must have merely waved in response, for Lorna didn't hear anything.

"He's so killer-awesome. Don't you think he's killer-awesome, Mom?"

"I think we've already covered that subject, honey." She couldn't keep the sigh from her words.

"I have a great idea. Why don't you marry *him?*"

Lorna staggered to a stop, positive her expression exhibited dismay. "Oh, Sam, don't even say that."

"Why not? He's—"

"I know. He's killer and awesome and whatever. But, well, first of all, he doesn't want to get married, and second of all, I don't, uh . . ." She didn't quite know how to tell her son that Clint was too much like Wild Bill, his dad.

She didn't want Sam to think his father had been anything but the fine, brave man she'd told him he was. She didn't want to have to say, *"Clint is a wild man, like your father was. Killer-awesome and nuts! Didn't you see how he almost killed himself out there just now? I won't do that to my heart again. I won't do it to yours."* Instead, she bit her lip, clasping him by the shoulders. "I— He's not my type, honey. Now let's not talk about it again. Okay?"

He looked dubious. "Dorks are your type?"

She bit her lip, forcing herself not to grin. "Do *not* use that word, and no, dor— Er, they aren't my type. You'll see. There are lots of guys here who aren't—aren't the *D* word, and who *are* my type."

"What is your type, Mom?"

She didn't intend to discuss this with him. She swatted his backside. "You're not sidetracking me, kiddo. You still have to take that bath. Now scoot. You have fifteen minutes to wash off that layer of muck, or I'll scrape you clean with a putty knife."

As Sam trotted off, she had the oddest tingling at the nape of her neck, as though someone were watching her. Not caring to think about who it might be, she quickened her pace.

An hour later, Lorna felt much better. She was clean and had food in her stomach, even if it was her own cooking. She checked her watch. Seven-thirty. Good, she was ready early. There'd be time to visit with Sam. It seemed as though their quality times were few and far between. Checking herself in the mirror for one last inspection, she shook out her froth of curls, still slightly damp from her shower.

The short pink sundress she'd chosen didn't look all that good with her lug-soled boots, but Barney's taste for shoe leather had given her little choice. She didn't know when she'd have time to shop for shoes; there'd been so much plumbing work keeping her busy. She only hoped Clyde didn't think she resembled Olive Oyl.

In a bout of déjà vu, she entered her pink living room to find the situation very similar to the way it had been the night before. Clint was lounging on her puce couch, looking quite at home. "Hi." He scanned her, grinning. "Nice shoes."

"Thanks." She ignored the flutter in her stomach and flounced down in the lumpy chair. "Barney doesn't seem to share your taste. They're the only ones he hasn't eaten."

"Is that true, buddy?" Clint leaned forward to flick the eraser on the end of a pencil the squirrel was gnawing. Barney glanced up and chattered for a few seconds before returning to his destructive pastime. Clint gave her a pseudoserious look. "He refuses to answer on the grounds that it may incriminate him."

Sam laughed, coming in from the kitchen with a plate of brownies. "He leaves his teeth marks in every pencil we have. It's sort of like his autograph."

"Well, he's left his autograph on a few too many of my shoes, too. I'm starting a collection of gourmet squirrel recipes."

"Odd how he hasn't dived into the brownies," Clint commented.

"Naw. He doesn't like Mom's brownies."

Clint grinned at her. "He'll eat shoes and pencils, but not your brownies? That's not a good sign."

Sam grabbed up one of the dark squares. "Well, they're a little gross, but they don't make me sick."

Lorna couldn't help but laugh. "It's a mother's dream to hear such high praise from her child."

"Want one?" Sam asked Clint, his cheeks bulging.

He grinned at the boy. "I'll pass."

"I dare you, Mr. I-Take-Dares-for-a-Living," Lorna said challengingly.

He glanced her way, looking fully into her eyes. His gaze was dazzling in its mirth. "That's cruel."

Barney was now scanning the dish, his nose twitching as he sniffed, but he made no move toward the food.

"Maybe I'll just try a pencil." Clint picked up the gnawed thing and examined it. "On second thought, I'm not very hungry."

Sam took another brownie and stuffed it in his mouth. "Gotta save some for ol' Clyde the dork."

"Sam!" Lorna reprimanded. "What did I tell you?"

He smirked, chewed, but made no reply.

"Clyde Canasta? He's your date?" Clint replaced the pencil and lazed back on the couch.

Lorna didn't like his laughing tone, or his relaxed way. How dare he treat her home as though it were his! *Even if it is?* her mind chided. "His name is Clyde *Simmons,* and yes, he's my date," she said thinly.

"He's a dork, isn't he, Clint?" Sam asked.

Brushing back an obstinate shock of hair, he shrugged. "Barney's the dork detector around here. I'd only be guessing." The ebony strand fell back across his forehead. The stuff was as willful as the man.

Lorna watched as the two exchanged knowing glances, and their easy camaraderie irritated her further. "Just what can we do for you, Mr. McCord?" She stood, suddenly restive. "Out of eggs again?"

Barney took that instant to jump into Clint's lap, causing his eyes to widen for a fraction of a second. Without regard for the sensitivity of certain parts of the male anatomy, Barney began to burrow. Clint winced. "Okay, Barn," he said, a little gruffly. "I know what you're after, and I haven't got any to spare." Plucking the animal from his quest, he deposited him on the cushion beside Sam.

Lorna found Clint's discomfort diverting, and couldn't hide her grin. "Are you okay?"

He cleared his throat, keeping a wary eye on Barney. "What was the question?"

"I asked if you were okay."

He glanced her way, his expression dubious. "No, the other question, smart stuff."

"Oh." She tried to straighten her face, but she was having a hard time. It was his turn to be embarrassed, and it felt good. "I think I was asking if you're out of nuts—I mean eggs."

He chuckled. "Good save. Actually, I'm here to get Sam for the Eastwood extravaganza I promised this afternoon. Bo rented two of his flicks."

"Yeah? Cool." Sam jumped up. "I'll sack up the brownies and take them with us. Maybe Bo'll eat one."

"The optimism of youth." Clint stood.

"They're very *good* brownies," she retorted, pretending affront.

"I'm sure. Just not quite as good as a pencil."

She shook her head at him, enjoying their banter. "I still dare you to taste one."

Sam disappeared into the kitchen with the plate, and Clint's gaze followed his departure. Apparently deciding the boy didn't need to hear him, he moved around the coffee table toward her. "Is that any way to treat somebody who's offered to baby-sit your kid?"

"But I thought you lived so dangerously," she taunted. Oh, lord, was she flirting? She hoped not. Her smile vanished.

He came closer, and in such a small room, that didn't leave her much space to escape. The scent of his after-shave was all around her, and she tried to take a protective step back, but the dratted lumpy chair held her hostage.

"What makes you so sure I live dangerously?"

"I—I saw you almost crash this afternoon." In desperation to put distance between them, she sat down.

"That was a close call." His gaze was intent, and for an instant she thought he was talking about something more recent than his death-defying maneuver in the sky. "And I still won't eat your brownies. Go figure." He smiled that sexy smile of his, and the breath left her body.

"I'm ready!" Sam reappeared holding up a plastic bag. "Mom, can I take Aunt Bee?"

She blinked, and jerked to look at her son. "Uh, sure. Just don't let her get lost."

"Aw, Mom. I won't."

She was immediately sorry she'd been overcritical, but Clint's closeness was stressing her out. "I know you won't." She smiled at him. "Have a good time."

"Can I have some gum?"

"In my toolbox." She gestured toward where it sat beside the couch.

As he rummaged, there was a knock at the door.

"Darn, I meant to be gone before your date got here," Clint said.

Deftly avoiding his touch, she vaulted up to answer the door, tossing him a *"sure you did"* frown.

"Hello, Clyde!" she shouted as she swung the door wide. "I'm so glad to see you."

The man on the front stoop seemed overwhelmed by the fervor of her greeting, for he took a step back.

"Hello, Lorna!" he yelled, apparently assuming she was hard of hearing.

Embarrassed, she took his hand and lowered her voice to normal. "Won't you come in?"

"Thanks," he said, still a little loud. "I think I will."

Clyde wasn't as tall as Lorna remembered him to be. Possibly because she'd spent her time with him crouching under his bathroom sink. Most people seemed taller when she was in that position. Clyde, as it turned out, was just a little taller than she. But he had a sturdy, boyish face and blond curly hair. He looked very much like one of those postage-stamp cherubs, grown-up and stuffed into a corduroy suit. "Ready to go?" he bellowed.

She blushed. "Uh, Clyde, I can hear you. You don't have to shout."

"Oh!" he yelled, then hesitated, repeating, "Oh—okay. I thought you mighta got some water in your ear and got it infected or something."

There was a throat-clearing from behind her, and Lorna remembered her manners. "No—no infection. Uh, Clyde, you know Clint McCord, my landlord. And this is my son, Sam." She turned, indicating them, in time to see her child jamming his finger down his throat, his eyes rolled back in their sockets. It was his "This guy is a dork" sign. The badly timed introduction caught him in the act.

"Oh, *gosh dang!*" Clyde said. "Your son's chokin'! But don't worry, I took a course."

Before anyone could stop him, Clyde was behind Sam, jerking his fists upward and inward under his rib cage. Sam was making grunting sounds when suddenly his gum rocketed across the room and slammed onto the opposite wall. It stuck there, a glob of gray on bright pink.

"Clyde!" she cried. "I—I think he's okay. You can stop." She wanted to spank Sam right then and there, but if she did, her date would have to know his status as a dork in the boy's eyes, so she simply glared at her son. "Are you okay?" she asked through gritted teeth.

He coughed and swallowed. "My—my gum . . ."

"Yeah," Clyde said, looking puffed up with lifesaving pride. "You musta got it stuck down your throat. Good thing I was here."

"Good thing," Clint echoed. Lorna could tell he was having a rough time keeping his composure. He ran a hand over his lips to hide their twitching. "I guess we'd better go, sport."

"Uh-huh." Sam lifted a chastened look to his mother.

"We'll discuss your...gum problem later," Lorna warned as he picked up Aunt Bee's cage. "Won't we, Sam?"

"Yes—ma'am." Knowing he was in big trouble, he cast his glance to the floor and headed toward the door.

"Say thank you to Mr. Simmons, Sam," she said.

Chewing his lip, he gave the beaming man a weak smile. "Thank you, sir."

"You're welcome, my boy. Just be careful in the future. Gum can be pretty dangerous. You know, it's not legal to bring it into Hong Kong or Singapore—someplace over there. I saw it on TV."

"They do a lot of choking on gum?" Clint prodded, and Lorna gave him a dark look. She hadn't known him long, but she knew he was a kidder. She would have bet a million dollars he was thinking all kinds of incorrigible and irreverent thoughts beneath that earnest expression. Anybody who would come within a second of crashing his own plane into the earth couldn't be too worried about Singapore's gum statutes.

"I think the law's because there's been a lot of sticking it on walls and under chairs and stuff."

Clint nodded, frowning thoughtfully. Lorna marveled at how he maintained his stoicism. She was having trouble, even as upset as she was with Sam.

"I'll be careful, sir." Sam was so miserable, Lorna could hardly stand to look at his puckered face. Still, he deserved a lecture and some sort of punishment. She'd have to think about that.

"Mind if I wash my hands?" Clyde asked as Sam shuffled out the door.

"Not at all." She indicated the kitchen. "It's the least I can do."

He walked out of their view, leaving Lorna and Clint to look at each other. To the accompaniment of running water, Clint ambled over to her, whispering, "In some primitive cultures, saving the chewing gum of a woman's son means the woman has to marry the man."

"That's not funny," she hissed under her breath.

"Are you sure?" His grin was cheeky.

She planted her hands on her hips, intent on glaring him down, but the absurdity of the situation, plus his incessant charm, got the better of her. She found herself grinning back. "Oh, you!" She swallowed an errant giggle. "I'm training Aunt Bee to kill sarcastic men. Be *very* afraid."

"Have a nice date, Mrs. Willow." As he walked away, he chuckled, and the rich sound tugged at her heart.

5

Lorna, Reva and Thelma had decided to meet for lunch
in the diner every day at noon. They concluded it would be
a good way to exchange information about the town and
its men, and just to do some meaningful female bonding
in a community awash in testosterone. Today, when Lorna
arrived, there was an extra woman at the table.

Reva looked up, and her big red lips parted in a smile.
"Yoo-hoo! We're back here."

The buxom nurse continued to wave and call out, as
though a table of three women in a diner full of men would
be hard to spot. Lorna nodded, wending her way to the
farthest table, which seemed to have become theirs—another concession the bachelors of Brazen Gulch had given
their newest female residents. Nice of them, she thought.
Too bad she wasn't finding any of her dates quite as perfect on a one-to-one basis as they seemed to be en masse.

"Hi." She smiled at the women, taking the only vacant
seat. "Sorry I'm late, but George Breakbone kept me
talking for a half hour."

Reva groaned. "About his frog collection?" When
Lorna nodded, the nurse rolled her eyes. "I had to *see* it
on our date Monday. All those dried-up things. The man's
a fiend."

"Frog fiend," Thel murmured, her eyes downcast. Then she giggled. Reva and the other woman joined in.

Lorna smiled, grateful she'd managed to get away before George forced her to look at his dried frogs. Her glance traveled to the new woman at the table, who was sitting directly across from Lorna. She had a heavy laborer's body, strapping and hard, but her face was lovely, with big, fawnlike brown eyes. Her hair was long, falling past her flannel-clad shoulders in soft waves of red-gold. She was smiling, displaying small, even teeth. Stretching out a sturdy arm, she said, "Hello. I'm Maggie Goode. New manager of the hardware store. Glad to finally meet you."

She took Lorna's fingers in hers; though the large woman was obviously strong, she had a completely feminine handshake. "Nice to meet you, Maggie."

"We were just discussing our latest *d-a-t-e-s,*" Reva confided as Mavis came up, chomping her gum loudly.

"What can I do ya for, hon?" Wetting the tip of her pencil with her tongue, she added, "Usual? Hold the onions?"

"Yes, thanks."

Lorna was startled when the waitress touched her shoulder. "Thanks again, hon, for the other night. Me and Joel had us a talk, and he ain't gonna do me that way again."

Lorna smiled in sympathy. "I was happy to help." She started to add *anytime,* but stopped herself, remembering her vow to stay out of crazy situations. She was making a new start here.

With a last, friendly pat on Lorna's shoulder, Mavis wiggled away.

"Well, as I was saying..." Reva leaned in so that she could speak in a conspiratorial whisper. "I went out with

Herm Humbolt last night. Any of you been out with Herm?''

The other heads shook. "Well, just be warned ahead of time." She paused for emphasis, her expression wide-eyed and animated. "He has a thing for naked *f-e-e-t!*"

Maggie sputtered in her coffee, and Thel gasped. Lorna wondered why Reva had spelled out *feet*.

"What do you mean, Reva? What does he do to them?" Thelma asked, taking an absentminded bite of her fruit salad.

The nurse sat back and adjusted her face into a bland mask as Mavis came over with coffee for Lorna. When the waitress was gone, she leaned forward again. "Well, he wants you to put them in his lap, and he *rubs* them."

Thelma gasped. "That's smutty."

"Well..." Reva grinned wickedly. "He's pretty good at it."

"Reva!" Thelma's whisper was horror-stricken. "You let the man do *things* to your feet?"

The nurse wagged her eyebrows. "He didn't do anything smutty, Thel. Just rubbed and...well...sucked a little."

"Heaven spare me!" Thelma's fork clanked to the table.

Maggie laughed, a thoroughly melodious sound. "A frog fiend and a toe-sucker. Sounds like a weird little burg we've moved to, ladies."

Lorna's sandwich came, but she'd lost her appetite. Not that there was anything so terrible about having your toes sucked, but after her date last night with the cherub in corduroy, she had to heave a sigh. Reva's story reminded her that she and Clyde hadn't hit it off, either. Somehow, she couldn't see herself defining her life as a canasta player—which was the sort of woman Clyde was searching for.

Whatever happened to simple, easy small talk, nature walks and discussions about good books? She and Clyde had played canasta with his mother and grandmother until one o'clock in the morning. If she never saw another deck of cards, she'd still manage to live a full life.

"What—? *What?*" Reva asked. "What's the big sigh for? What happened to you?"

Lorna shook her head. "Nothing so exciting as your story." She took a sip of her coffee. "I just found out I'm lousy at canasta and will probably never have another date with Clyde."

"Clyde Canasta!" Maggie said though a bite of hamburger. "I've heard of that nut, and I'm staying way, way clear. My ex was a bridge maniac. No more cardplayers for this wised-up woman."

"I have a date with him tomorrow," Thelma said quietly. "I like cards."

"Well, more power to you, Thel," Reva said with a thumbs-up gesture. "I hear he's pretty cute. Is he?"

Thelma's cheeks pinkened. "He's just dreamy. And a great dresser." She lifted her eyes to Lorna. "To be honest, I'm relieved to hear you two didn't hit it off. You're so pretty."

Now it was Lorna's turn to be embarrassed, and she had to laugh. "Oh, sure. Especially in my hip boots while I'm wading around in raw sewage. I'm just dreamy, too."

"Lord almighty," Maggie enthused under her breath, looking above Lorna's head toward the front of the diner. "Who's that hunk of man-meat who just came in?"

Since her back was to the door, Lorna allowed Reva and Thelma to gawk at the hunk.

"Oh, that's Clint McCord," Reva whispered, the revelation not surprising Lorna very much. "He's the best-looking man in town, Maggie. You're going to have to get in line for *h-i-m!*"

Thelma cocked her blond head inquisitively. "I don't know the man who's with him. Do you, Reva?"

The nurse frowned in thought. "No. New to me." Her lips spread in a big red grin. "I don't think it'll be long before we know, though. They're heading back here. Scrunch over, girls. Let's squeeze them in."

Lorna took a bite of her sandwich, wishing she hadn't just started her lunch. Even if she ate like a shark in a feeding frenzy, she couldn't finish before they got back here.

"Hi," came Clint's familiar voice, much too near Lorna's ear.

She looked up and swallowed, but before she could answer, Reva was on her feet. "Here, guys, we're making room. You will join us, won't you?"

"Sure," he said.

Lorna closed her eyes and took another bite of her sandwich, trying to hurry as Clint got a chair from a nearby table and slipped it between her and Reva. The other man, Lorna instantly realized, must be Bo. He had a full flaming red beard and a bush of matching hair. He was as tall as Clint, but weighed close to a hundred pounds more. A mountain of a man. She didn't know if they could squeeze his bulk in, but it was clear Maggie planned to try. She'd quickly retrieved a chair, and she was showing Bo to it. "Here, Clint," she was saying. "You sit by me."

Clint, who'd just seated himself, looked up. "Thanks, but I'm already sitting."

Maggie looked over at him, confused. "Your name's Clint, too?"

"He's Clint. I'm Bo. Bo Pickett." The big man's voice was soft for his size, and his smile was dazzling through all that red. Lorna had never seen him up close, and she decided Bo was a strikingly handsome man, if you liked big red bear types. Which Maggie clearly did.

"Oh." Maggie giggled. "Misunderstanding. I asked who the hunk was when you came in, and everybody thought I meant Clint, I guess."

"Go figure." Bo winked at Clint. "Sorry, pal. Guess I'm the hunk today."

Clint chuckled. "What's the world coming to?"

Lorna crossed her legs, but it seemed impossible to get away from Clint's touch. They were just too crammed together.

He nudged Lorna's arm, whispering, "Who thought I was a hunk?" When she snapped around to frown at him, he asked, "Not you, huh?" He shot her that bothersome grin. "How did I know that?"

She wanted to retort, but couldn't, having just taken a bite of food.

"Before you swallow and get after me about leaving Sam alone, he's in Sheriff Andy's office, playing with Opie."

She stared at him, finally managing to swallow. "You're kidding."

"Yeah, I'm kidding. Since you grounded him for the gum episode, we knew you wouldn't let him eat in town, but we couldn't leave him, so he's bound and gagged in the trunk of the car."

His dusky eyes twinkled, and she knew he was lying, so she decided to go along. "That's just as well—it's pretty crowded in here."

Thelma inhaled, in shock, and Lorna realized the poor woman probably wasn't a devotee of satire. "He's teasing, Thel." She faced Clint. "Where is he, really?"

"He's really in the sheriff's office," Bo interjected. "Taking back the Eastwood tapes and picking out a couple more."

Lorna frowned in confusion.

"The sheriff's real name is Abner. He has five sons and is a widower," Clint said. "If any of you are interested in a ready-made basketball team, he's your man."

"He also has the local tape rental outlet," Bo explained. "Since there isn't much crime here, he decided to branch out."

Clint shifted, and when he did, his arm brushed hers. A wanton thrill raced through her as he joked, "Nobody's ever late returning rented tapes. The fine is forty-eight hours in jail."

Reva, Maggie and Bo laughed. Thelma's little eyes grew wide with horror. Lorna took a nervous bite of her sandwich, still wanting to get away. They were crushed too close together for her peace of mind. Clint's after-shave was hypnotic, giving her an urge to snuggle against his chest, draw those pesky, sexy lips to hers and . . . and . . .

"Lorna!" Reva fairly shouted, jerking her back from nutso-fantasyland.

"What?"

"Where did you go? I was saying our landlady has the cutest little daughter. She's around ten, and her name's Pansy or something."

"Patsy," Thelma corrected.

"Oh, yeah. Anyway, maybe you could get Patsy and Sam together for a *d-a-t-e.*"

Lorna blanched. The idea of Sam doing anything that needed to be spelled made her shiver. "Uh, I'm sure Sam would love to meet the local kids. But I don't think he's ready to date."

"There's a local 4-H group," Bo said. "As a matter of fact, they have a summer day camp. Maybe Sam would like to join in."

Lorna was startled to hear that, but pleasantly so. "Really? He could meet the other kids?"

"I think Patsy's in it," Thelma said. "She said something about camp last night at dinner."

"Sam would love to get involved in camp." Lorna was excited. This would solve her baby-sitting problem.

"They're holding camp at Roger's farm, just outside of town. If you want, I can take him by after lunch and see if he'd like it," Bo said. "They do crafts and learn to grow things, cook and whatnot."

"Cook?" Lorna smiled wanly. "I could use a good cook around the house."

Clint chuckled, and she gave him a look.

"What?" he asked, feigning innocence, as though spinach meat loaf and brownies that tasted worse than pencils hadn't flitted across his mind.

"You are *so* transparent." She shifted her leg away from his again, deciding the less attention she paid to him the better. She took another bite of her sandwich as Mavis came up.

"Hi, Sugar Hips and Big Red." She smoothed out an imaginary wrinkle across one full hip. "Here to sweet-talk me, or do you wanna eat?"

"Sweet-talk, darlin'," Clint teased. "But as long as we're here, bring me a roast beef on wheat and iced tea."

"Ditto," Bo said. "But make that two roast beefs and a jug of tea. I'm a little hungry."

"Got it. Normal for Hips and Berserko Platter for Red."

"Sugar *Hips?*" Lorna asked, unable to help herself.

"There was this contest last month." He winked. "You can call me Sugar."

She shook her head at him in amused exasperation. "You can hold your breath."

Forcing her attention to other things, she noticed that Maggie and Bo were engaged in a private conversation. Both were grinning oddly and looking deeply into each other's eyes. Two very big, very attractive people, all alone in a crowd. She had a feeling she'd been a lucky witness to that elusive romantic entity called love at first sight, and that Maggie Goode and Bo Pickett would be one of Brazen Gulch's first newspaper-advertisement-induced weddings. She couldn't help but smile, happy for them both.

"Why are you smiling?" Clint uttered, as an aside.

She shifted, only to find his lips very near her own. Her reaction was so strong, she couldn't speak.

His gaze held hers for a long, scary minute as he seemed to try to get into her mind. Finally, he indicated the couple in question with a nod. "They are cute, aren't they?"

Her cheeks blazing, she spun away. He was a perceptive man. Maybe too perceptive. She wondered if he knew she was having trouble keeping her hands off him, and if it tickled him as much as his amused eyes seemed to suggest.

"Hi, Mom," came Sam's voice at her back. He didn't sound as exuberant as usual, and she knew why. He was grounded, and he was supposed to be shining his shoes, cleaning Aunt Bee's cage and washing all the cabin windows, inside and out.

"Hi, yourself. Get some movies?"

She turned to him as he shrugged and mumbled, "I put 'em in the Jeep."

"How'd the morning go?"

His expression was hangdog and he didn't quite meet her eyes. "I got everything done but two windows. Clint said they couldn't leave me alone."

She took his hand and squeezed, taking pity on him. "Clint was right. How would you like to meet some of the kids who live here?"

He brightened. "When?"

"This afternoon. There's a summer day camp. You'll do crafts and stuff—maybe even cook."

"Cook?" He looked doubtful.

"I think they do milk shakes," Clint said.

"No kiddin'?" His puckered forehead smoothed.

Clint sat back to better see the boy, placing a casual arm across the edge of Lorna's chair. "And chili dogs. Maybe even ice-cream sodas."

"Oh, fine. Junk food," Lorna moaned.

"Hey, it's a day camp, not Cholesterol Counters of America," Clint reminded her with a laugh, touching her shoulder.

She stiffened. "I suppose," she breathed. It came out husky. Twisting in the chair to slip away from Clint's touch, she squeezed Sam's fingers again. "I've got to get back to work. Take my seat." She pushed her chair away from the table and stood, feeling a little unsteady. Fishing in her pocket, she drew out a ten-dollar bill and held it toward Clint, grateful her fingers didn't shake. "This is for mine and Sam's. Would you mind paying Mavis?"

He eyed the bill. "I never take money from women."

"What about tenants?" She dropped the ten on the table, then turned to Bo, who was still talking in low, confidential tones to Maggie, oblivious of everything else. Not wanting to interrupt the lovebirds, she looked at Clint again, with great hesitancy. "Would—would you thank Bo for me, for taking Sam to the day camp?"

He nodded. "If he comes up for air. If he doesn't, I'll drop Sam off."

She smiled in gratitude. His answering grin made her weak in the knees, the bum.

Lorna wasn't particularly looking forward to her date tonight, but after all the bad news she had to give Stu Littleman about his plumbing, she hadn't had the heart to refuse. After thinking about it, she decided the date might work in her favor. If he tried anything, she could just warn him it was either hands off or he could shower in fire hydrants for the rest of his life. She wasn't above blackmail, when it came to groping men.

When she came out of her bedroom, ready for her date, she stumbled to a halt when she saw Clint on her couch, feeding raisins to Barney. He looked good, all broad shoulders and long legs—and that perpetually tousled hair that beckoned a woman's hands to smooth and caress it. She could even detect his sexy after-shave. He was a cruel man.

Chewing the inside of her cheek, she looked around. Sam was nowhere to be seen, so she demanded, "Who do you think you are, my father?"

He looked up with a grin. "Not even in my sickest fantasies."

She blushed. "Save it for your therapist. Where's Sam?"

He shrugged, offering Barney another raisin. "Beats me. I thought he was yours. I came over to get him—"

"He's missing?" she cried.

"Maybe he's talking to Bo."

She hurried to the door and threw it open. *"Sam!"* Her voice was shrill with panic. "Sam, where are you?"

"Coming!" came a distant voice.

She saw him then, just heading out of the hangar, the orange of the setting sun turning his blond hair fiery as he dashed across the flower-strewn field. Relief rushed through her. "Thank goodness."

"Look, kids his age like to—"

"I know." She slumped against the wall. "I know, I'm too protective." It was only then that she realized he had stood and was coming over to her. His jeans were pressed and creased, his knit shirt was a pristine white. Clearly he was spiffed up, ready to go out and rock some woman's world.

He leaned a shoulder against the wall, very near. "Sam's a good kid, Lorna. Don't give yourself a nervous breakdown about him."

She eyed him with misgiving. "Yes, I know. 'Don't worry, Lorna. Nothing will happen. Everything will be okay.'" She pushed herself away from the wall to put distance between them. "I've heard it all before."

The door banged open, and Sam burst inside. "Sorry, Mom." He panted. "I was helping Bo clean up the hangar, and then the phone rang and it was a message for you."

"Me?" She ran her hand through her curls in dejection. "Who's sprung a leak this time?"

"Mr. Littleman."

She was confused. "My date?"

Sam shook his head. "No. He said his mildew allergy is kicking up and he's got a migraine and he's going to bed."

"Oh." She was amazed at the satisfaction that flooded her, and found herself feeling like smiling. She hadn't realized how much she didn't want to go out with Stu Littleman until this minute. "Well, kiddo, that leaves more time for us. I'll just call the baby-sitter and cancel."

Sam's face didn't brighten.

"What's wrong, honey?"

He shrugged his hands into his baggy jeans pockets. "Aw, at lunch Clint invited me to the movies. It's Cyber Alien Empire. It's Disney! You said I could see it when it came out."

She swung her gaze to the man, and he shrugged. "I didn't realize you'd found a baby-sitter."

"Let me go, Mom," Sam begged, his face screwed up with anxiety.

She didn't want to disappoint him, but she didn't like the idea of these two bonding any tighter than they already had.

"You can tag along," Clint told her. When she looked at him, he was smiling that smile that made her go numb inside. "If you don't talk during the picture, that is. I hate that in a tenant."

Knowing she was a fool, but also knowing she was going to accept, she exhaled in defeat. "How can I refuse such a gallant invitation?" In a last-ditch attempt to keep him at an emotional arm's length, she insisted, "We'll go Dutch, of course."

"Of course," he said. "You're the rich plumber."

She smiled outright then. Damn his easygoing charm. "I need to call the sitter."

"On the way to the car, I'll tell Bo to call her."

Since the plans seemed to be made, she turned to her son, fondly touching his cheek. "Honey, you'd better change that shirt. And wash your hands, too."

"I'll be right back." Grinning, he sprinted into the bedroom.

She sat down on the couch, giving Clint her reluctant attention. "How do you happen to be free this evening? Or have you already been *tamed* today?"

He strolled over and sat down beside her. "I took three women flying this afternoon, so I'm tired of being tamed."

"I see." She inspected his profile as he settled on the couch, unable to decide whether he was kidding or not. She had to assume he wasn't. Looking at him, it wasn't hard to believe the man could satisfy three women in one afternoon. She felt oddly grudging about that. "Just remember, I have no intention of taming you."

"Relax, Mrs. Willow." He lounged backward, facing her. "I invited your son to the movies, not you. Remember? Bo invited Maggie over, so I figured I'd make myself scarce." He stretched an arm across the back of the couch, his hand grazing her hair. "You can back out if you're afraid."

"Afraid? Ha!" She looked pointedly away, so that he couldn't see the panic in her eyes. Even the slight brush of his arm was making her insides all melty. She saw movement and spotted Barney dragging a sock across the floor. "Oh, Barn..."

"I hate that, too, when my squirrel is late with the laundry."

She rubbed her eyes. "He steals socks to make his nest. Half the time I can't find an entire pair."

"So that's the reason you're wearing one blue sock and one brown one."

She jerked forward to look. Sure enough, he was right. She hadn't even realized. The bedroom walls were so dark it was hard to see. Moaning, she sagged back. "I now have no matching socks. You all go on to the movie without me."

It startled her to hear him chuckle. "The first minute I saw you, a squirrel was digging for nuts on your head and you still managed to give me a 'go to hell' look."

She peered at him. "What is *that* supposed to mean?"

He took her by the hand, urging her upward. "It means, let's go, squirrel woman. Sam's coming."

6

When they entered Brazen Gulch's only movie theater, they noticed a commotion at the snack counter.

"Hmmm." Clint looked thoughtful.

"What?" Puzzled, Lorna followed his glance.

"The girl behind the counter seems upset."

Lorna could see her through the grumbling crowd. The teenage girl was brushing at a tear. Tall and reedy, with her cornsilk hair pulled back in a single braid, she whimpered, "I'm—I'm sorry. I just can't fix it."

"Oh, *fine,* Selma!" one patron bellowed. "This piece of junk never works. What about us people who want popcorn?"

Lorna recognized the man as Joe, her first date. Apparently this evening wasn't going too well for him. He was clutching a chunky brunette by the arm. Probably one of the many females who'd crammed into Brazen Gulch after reading the ad. The woman didn't look happy, either.

Lorna glanced at the beleaguered teen. The poor kid was completely out of her element and looking forlorn. "Sam, honey, you and Clint go on and find some seats." She patted her son on the shoulder. "I'll be right there."

"Okay, Mom. Hey!" He turned back to her, his expression blossoming in a grin. "There's Howie and Mac—

I met them at camp today." He pointed to a couple of boys waving near the door. "Can I sit with them?"

"Sure, sport," Clint said. "Meet us out here when it's over."

Lorna eyed Clint, rankled that he had answered for her. She started to say something about just whose child Sam was, but somebody else was giving Selma a bad time now, so she let it go. He'd only told Sam what she was about to say, anyway. "Excuse me a minute. You go on in."

"What are you doing?"

"Nothing for you to worry about."

Without looking back, she headed toward the snack bar. "Selma?" She worked her way to the front of the crowd. "If you have some tools, I think I can fix that for you." Her mind was berating her: *Here you go again, Lorna! Why can't you just stay out of it?* But, in her heart she knew it would be mean to leave this miserable girl at the mercy of snarling, popcorn-deprived moviegoers when she could do something about it.

The teenager blinked damp blue eyes at Lorna. "Huh? Tools? Yeah. There's a screwdriver and a wrench back here. I—I think that's what they are."

Lorna smiled. "That'll be fine."

Selma swiped at another tear, her freckled face brightening. "Thanks, uh, lady..." She lifted a section of the speckled linoleum counter, and Lorna stepped behind it.

"Lorna Willow," she told the girl, then faced the crowd. "Okay, folks, there'll be popcorn in a few minutes."

Hunkering down on her knees, she looked under the counter at the popcorn machine's works.

"Need some help?"

She almost fell over, she was so startled to find Clint kneeling beside her.

"I'm pretty handy," he told her.

She stared at him. "Don't bother. Go on in and watch the movie."

"Maybe with me helping, we can both watch the movie." He pulled the machine's plug from its electrical outlet.

She couldn't argue his point, so she just shrugged. "Maybe..." Though she tried to act nonchalant, she hadn't planned on him joining her in such cramped quarters.

Still, it would be faster with them both working. And from the sound of the crowd on the other side of the counter, the faster they got popcorn flowing, the less likely it was that there would be mob violence in downtown Brazen Gulch.

He scanned the wires and gear, commenting, "I thought you were a plumber."

"My dad was a regular Mr. Fix-It. Taught me about mechanical things."

"Hmmm." He held out a hand. "Wrench."

She hesitated handing it to him. "Really, I can do this."

His gaze moved to her face. "I have no doubt you can, Mrs. Willow." Lifting the tool from her fingers, he made an adjustment. "Screwdriver." He held the wrench out for her to take.

"This was my idea, remember?" She slid under the counter beside him. "I'll get it."

He had to scoot over to make room. "Be my guest."

Trying to overlook the amusement in his voice, she slithered on her back, grateful for the dry carpeting. That was a luxury in her business. It didn't occur to her until she was under there with Clint that he was lounging very near, his face not far above hers. "Okay, Mr. Fix-It's daughter. Go for it." His eyes were oddly radiant in the dark space.

Forcing her glance away, she scanned the workings of the machine, immediately seeing the problem. Her fingers were strangely clumsy, and it took her an extra few seconds to tighten the wire connection. "There," she said, sounding as if she'd just run a marathon. "That should do it."

"It should," he murmured.

He was leaning on one elbow, his face near hers, his breath warm against her cheek. Somehow he seemed nearer than he had a few seconds before. Her heart hammered erratically.

"Uh, we're done." She shifted to plug it in. Unfortunately, she had to shift in his direction to do it.

"Can I try it now?" Selma called from above.

His lips twitched. "Right." The girl switched on the machine, assuming he'd answered her. Somehow, Lorna didn't think he'd even heard the question.

She frowned at him in dismay. She shouldn't be here, but she couldn't seem to move. She could only stare, mesmerized, his nearness locking up her brain. Lord, he was handsome, grinning that infuriating grin, his black eyes sparkling like a night full of stars. That unruly hair, crying out to be touched, only inches from her face. And his scent, like a moonlit wood, beckoned, taunted....

It happened suddenly—mutual invitation and consent, all in the crazy flash of a second. He took her gently in his arms at the same instant she grasped his broad shoulders, relishing his lean, hard muscle beneath her fingers. As his lips took possession of hers, her response was instantaneous and primitive, her naked desire shameless, and she moved suggestively against him. She'd known this brand of wild abandon in a man's arms only once before—with only one other man.

That was a bad sign, but she couldn't stop herself. Clint's kiss, wildly masculine and disturbingly sweet, rocked her, and if she hadn't already been on her back, she would have fallen. A sound of awe escaped her throat, and she opened her lips fully, inviting the glorious invasion of his tongue.

The silken sensations he elicited in her were both thrillingly familiar and deliciously foreign. The sexual electricity they shared was overpowering, and his knowing hands burned where they touched, branding his imprint on her body.

She molded herself against him, feeling the raging heat of his arousal against her thigh. She wished she could stop herself, wished he didn't have the power to drive her crazy this way. But even more desperately she wanted to touch him, hold him, know him completely. The urge grew unbearable, and she began to snake her hand down, down—

There was a sound, an odd titter, and it pulled her partly from her drugged state. What was that?

"Hell..." Clint muttered against her lips.

His rough curse snapped her fully back, and she became aware of where she was and what she was doing. *Had she gone completely off her rocker?*

"Oh, my Lord..." She was so full of adrenaline, her body ached and shivered for fulfillment. She hated herself for that. Hated him. Shaking her head and trying to deny what had just happened, she shoved at his chest. "How could you?"

"Hell," he muttered again. "I'm sorry— It just..." He cursed again, and backed off, leaving her feeling foolishly bereft and alone.

She knew what he'd started to say. That it had just happened. That was the truth. And she also knew she'd *allowed* it. Even welcomed it. He probably hadn't realized it was going to happen any more than she had. Or if he had, he hadn't expected it to become more than a mischievous brush of lips. Damn.

Another noise intruded, besides the tittering laughter. It was the popping sound of a working popcorn machine, and a rousing cheer welled up from the assembled crowd.

Selma squatted down, her cheeks glowing with girlish enthusiasm. "It's working." She giggled, her eyes on Clint. "You'll have to teach me that." Covering her mouth with her hand to quell another bout of laughter, she stood, needing to get to work.

Clint sat up, raking a hand thought his hair. "It seems you've inspired another Miss Fix-It," he muttered.

"Oh, *please.*" She pushed up with a shaky arm. "The last thing on that girl's mind was popcorn machines. She was talking to you." Ignoring his offer of a hand up, she stood. "I'm out of the mood for snacks." She steadied herself against the counter, glaring down at him. "You go ahead and get something. I'm going in."

"I'm not interested in food." He retrieved the tools and stood, opening the counter to allow her to precede him. Grateful moviegoers, unaware of what had gone on beneath the counter, shook her hand and patted her shoulder, murmuring their thanks, but she hardly noticed. She tried not to be aware of Clint's movements, but even with her back to him, she knew where he was and what he was doing. Her female antennae were up and receiving.

She ran trembly fingers across her lips. They were still tingling. Upset to the point of hysteria, she found herself spinning to confront him. "Don't you ever *dare* do that again, Clint McCord!" she whispered harshly.

"I'd reword that, Mrs. Willow." There was no longer any laughter in his eyes, and his jaw was working. "Remember, I take dares for a living."

"I know that! And you know I'm not interested in a relationship with *you*. So if you ever come at me with those lips again, you can expect to wash dishes in a ten-foot geyser of water for the rest of your natural life." She jabbed him in the chest with a finger. "Is that clear?"

He took her offending hand and aimed her toward the door that led to the darkened theater. "Knee me in the groin next time, Mrs. Willow. It'll help remind me."

Clint stared at the screen as slimy aliens wreaked havoc in cyberspace to a booming, surrealistic orchestration, but he saw and heard none of it. His mind was on one little plumber with a quirky need to help people, and the hottest damned kiss this side of whatever virtual galaxy the alien fighters were warping around in.

Hell. He'd never been kissed that way before. Maybe it was her very quirkiness that made her so uninhibited at lovemaking. He lost track of the time as his brain kept drifting off into fantasies of having wild sex with the woman beside him. It wasn't giving his body any peace. He was damned glad the theater was dark and nobody could see the telltale bulge in his jeans.

He glanced at her. She was canted so far away from him, the woman on her other side must think she was trying to steal her gumdrops. Even so, her scent drifted around him, tormenting, making him stir uncomfortably in his seat. She didn't wear perfume. Her aroma was more like something baking, spicy and warm. He couldn't quite place it, but it was as seductive as anything he'd ever run across. And he'd run across a bunch.

Annoyed, he rested his elbow on the chair arm next to her. She reacted the way he'd expected—by slanting even farther away. It aggravated him to discover he was uncommonly attracted to her, and her continued rebuffs galled him. He wasn't used to it.

Damn it to hell, he could tell she wanted him as badly as he wanted her. And he wanted her badly. He closed his eyes, fighting another bout of lust. At least that was what he chose to call what he was feeling. Even so, he had a bad premonition that making love to this woman would mean more to him than just sex.

And families were a trap.

Shifting away, he swore under his breath. So an affair was out of the question. Falling for Lorna Willow was the *last* thing he planned to do.

Sunday evening rolled around with the speed of a slithering slug. As a matter of fact, that was exactly what Lorna's date reminded her of. Sweaty, ponderous, and slow-witted to boot. Ugh. He'd mistaken the word *plumber* for *hooker* and been all over her within fifteen minutes of her climbing into his pickup.

She'd had to use a self-defense trick her father had taught her years ago, and she was afraid Mr. Slug's ears would be ringing for a few days. But he would live. His plumbing might suffer, though, for she didn't plan to get within one hundred yards of the man unless he was tied to a tree.

Anyway, for once, she was back early from a date, even if she'd had to hitch a ride with a carload of women who'd spent an apparently satisfying weekend in Brazen Gulch and were on their way back to Oklahoma with stories of wild cowboys and hot Texas nights.

She experienced a surge of selfishness at the thought that Sam had started to make friends in town and was spending the night with his new buddy, Mac Healy. Mrs. Healy had offered to drop both boys off at camp the next morning, so Lorna was alone. And she felt it.

Usually, walking in the moonlight on a warm summer evening lifted her spirits. But not tonight. Nobody was at the air school, either—not that she had the urge to visit. In just a few days Bo and Maggie had become a real item and were always together. She didn't know where they were tonight, but they weren't in the building. No lights were on, at least. She supposed since they were lovers in the first heat of passion, the lack of lights didn't mean they weren't there. The erotic vision that popped into her brain made her blush, and she cast around for less titillating thoughts. Too bad the only picture that came to mind was of Clint's face.

Her flush deepened. She supposed he was still in Amarillo, at the air show. He'd flown out Friday morning. She hadn't seen him since they'd gone to the movies on Wednesday. That, at least, had been a blessing. The man had a way of getting under her skin, and she'd found out just how far and fast he could do it while they were under the popcorn machine. Her cheeks sizzled at the memory.

She headed aimlessly toward a copse of trees at the far end of the runway. In the moonlight, their leafy branches bowed and beckoned in the night wind. It was a lovely evening. Cool for late July. The moon was high, and even though it wasn't full, the clear, clean air made the night very bright.

She wore a short sundress that billowed and danced in the breeze. Tall grasses and wildflowers grazed her legs as she moved. Feeling slightly renewed by nature's soft beauty, she bent to pick a yellow blossom. As she meandered along, she lifted it to her nose. There was no true flowery scent, just a kind of dusty sweetness. Much nicer than Mr. Slug's cloying after-shave.

She reached the trees, and paused at the wood's edge to lean against the rough bark of a spindly oak. Closing her eyes, she inhaled the night scents. She liked Brazen Gulch. Liked the people—well, except for every single date she'd had so far. But surely there was a nice solid man here she could love, who would be a good daddy for Sam.

From work and on dates, she'd gotten to know only twenty or twenty-five of the local men, so far. There were a couple hundred eligible bachelors. Surely among them was *one* nice, normal guy. "Where are you?" she murmured, and was startled at the desperation in her tone. She had a panicky feeling she knew why the unhappiness was there. She was afraid if she didn't find an ordinary, sane man soon, Clint might find himself welcomed into her bed and her heart. That would never do. Not another reckless, sexy rogue!

"I'm over here," came a quiet, male voice. "Or were you talking to me?"

She jerked up, scanning the dark glade. She saw nothing but shadowy shanks of trees. "Clint?" she breathed. "What are you doing out here?" She sensed movement, then saw him when he stood. As her eyes adjusted to the deep shade, she could make out a bedroll. "Why are you sleeping in the woods?"

"Bo left a note on the door. Apparently Maggie likes playing naked chase-me games, so I figured I'd bed down out here for the night." He indicated the bedroll. "Want to sit?"

She hadn't seen Bo's car. Maybe it had been hidden behind her truck. She supposed she hadn't been paying much attention. She knew she should make an excuse and escape, but she was oddly reluctant to do so, and could only shake her head at his offer. "Why—why aren't you sleeping in the hangar?"

"I like the night." He sat back down and leaned against the tree. "Apparently you do, too."

"Yes." The breeze ruffled her hair and toyed with the hem of her dress in a gesture that seemed to coax her to join him. Or did it? She swallowed, watching transfixed as he wrapped an arm about one bent knee. He was fully dressed in boots, jeans and a dark knit shirt. She was thankful for that.

"How was your date?"

She sagged against the oak, wrapping an arm about the trunk. She was *not* going over there to him! "Uh, short. How was Amarillo?"

"Long." He grinned. "Made some money, though."

"And you're not even dead. Congratulations."

He looked at her for a long minute, then ran a contemplative hand across his chin. "Want to fly?"

She blanched, clasping the tree with both hands. Her knees were suddenly mush. "Uh, you mean—" she indicated the air with a lift of her chin "—up there?"

White teeth flashed in the darkness. "That's usually where it's done. Why? Did you have something else in mind?"

She shook her head. "No— I mean, no, I don't want to fly—anywhere."

His grin didn't dim. "Okay." He stretched out his legs, crossing them at the ankles. "Nice night."

She nodded.

"Where's Sam?"

"Staying with Mac Healy."

He nodded, thoughtfully pursing his lips.

The silence grew between them, but Clint seemed to be at ease. Totally relaxed. She, on the other hand, was clinging to the tree as though it were the last handhold between her and a painful, prolonged death in a chasm full of slithering cobras. She searched her mind for a possible subject they could chat about, but blanked out. In her frenzied attempt, her brain caught upon a topic, and it leaped to her lips. "You—you know what you need?"

He canted his head, his grin reappearing. "Yep." Lacing his fingers behind his head, he watched her closely. "But I'd be curious to hear your opinion."

Oh, Lord, there was that grin again! She couldn't imagine why she didn't turn and run, but for some reason her legs refused to obey her orders. She feigned nonchalance. "You need a llama."

He stared at her for a second, then chuckled. "That would have been my second guess."

"No—no, really. I've always thought if I ever had any property I'd get a couple of llamas. They're great pets. You can even bring them in the house. And if you had a flock of sheep, llamas are better than dogs as guards. And they don't even need special food."

"The dogs or the sheep?" he asked, rising to his feet.

"No—the llamas."

"I see." He began to walk toward her. The way he moved was thrilling to watch. Her brain went all fuzzy, but she babbled on. "Llamas graze. They eat all kinds of grass. So...so no more lawn mower. You could even use their wool to make clothes and blankets."

"Um-hmm." He came up to her and took her hand.

She tugged at his hold. "What are you doing?"

"I'm listening. Go on."

"Oh..." She fought off a surge of dizziness. "Well, they can carry supplies, too. One thing, though, they spit when they're upset, naturally—"

"Naturally."

He was leading her toward the bedroll, and she didn't seem able to find the willpower to fight it. Her brain was on an odd sort of automatic pilot, and all she could manage to do was blather on. "But they—they usually don't spit except at each other, and that's over food."

"Of course it is." He sat down on the blanket, pulling her with him. When he leaned toward her, she felt an electric sparkle in her core. "Now, Mrs. Willow, let's talk about what we *both* need."

She took a quick, stunned breath, tilting backward on her elbows. "No—we don't need anything."

"Then why did you stand there pitching like a used llama salesman? You could have left anytime."

"I... I..." She swallowed. She didn't know why! Didn't have a good, sound answer. "I—was trying to help...."

"Okay. Thank you." He leaned closer. "Now, I'm going to kiss you—out of gratitude."

He lowered his face to within an inch of hers, then stopped, a half grin playing on his lips. "If you're going to knee me, do it now." His eyes expressed more challenge than fear. "I won't wait long."

The breeze brushed a shank of his hair against her forehead. Though the touch was nothing more than an airy caprice of the night wind, the fleeting union set her skin aglow. As though in a trance, she reached up to smooth it. The stuff was silken and strangely warm against her fingers.

Taking her hand, he kissed her palm, his tongue teasing with feathery strokes. The intimacy in his taste of her flesh was another very small thing; still, she was lost. "Kiss me..." She slid her hands to his nape, tugging him down to blanket her body. "We'll do this once...just once...." she told herself in a sigh. "Then we'll never do it again. Promise?"

"Just show me where to sign, sweetheart," he muttered huskily.

She opened her mouth with a small whimper, but when their tongues met and mingled, her helpless melancholy sizzled away like water on a burning skillet. His kiss held a staggering male hunger that unnerved her, sending jolt after jolt of desire through her. She felt deliriously crushed by his warm, virile nearness. He was so big, so alive, her entire universe. His body felt right pressed into hers, and she throbbed with the need to be naked in his arms, to cry out in pure, gasping passion as he buried himself in her softness, plunging his hard strength deep inside her.

He groaned, settling himself so that she could feel the full heat of him between her legs. The sensation was heaven on earth, and she rubbed against him, eliciting another groan as he lifted his lips from hers. His kisses trailed along her cheek to nibble at her ear. "Would you be offended if I kissed you there?"

"In my ear?" she breathed raggedly.

"No."

She smiled in realization, wanton laughter gurgling in her throat. "I dare you."

"Oh...baby..." His chuckle rippled through her as he slowly, seductively slipped lower, ever lower. Unbuttoning her dress as he went, he pleasured her with his tongue and his hands as he moved.

She didn't know how it happened, for sanity became a distant acquaintance once his lips began to bring her body alive, but she became aware of the fact that she was devoid of clothes—and so was he.

He was a beautiful, naked animal. And he knew exactly how to gratify a woman. His hands were delving into intimate recesses, teasing, exciting. She snuggled deeper into the crook of his arm. "You should never wear clothes," she said through a passion-drenched sigh.

He lifted his gaze to her face, a crooked grin on those talented lips. "I shouldn't?"

She closed her eyes, enjoying his stroking. "Covering that body is a crime." He kissed the top of her head in answer. When his fingers explored more deeply, she gasped. "And you should do *that* for a living. I like it."

"I must not be doing it very well. I wanted you to love it," he murmured.

"Oh— *Oh...*" She arched involuntarily as starbursts lit the sky.

"Oh, what?" he queried.

She kissed his chest, teasing the crisp mat of hair with her tongue. "I—I'm dying."

"Ah. That's better."

She smiled, opening herself further to him. "You're killing me," she said with a sigh.

"Mmmmm..."

His hands worked wicked magic, and the honeyed heat of her climax rushed through her, taking her away from the bedroll and the dark glade to a place where she had never thought she would travel again. She spiraled and soared in pure, wild ecstasy.

She clung to him, shaking, reeling in sexual gratification. Yet she was oddly discontented, for he had not yet taken her as a man takes a woman—not wholly, completely. Her need for him was wild and primitive, and she clawed at his back, kissed his neck, his jaw. "Don't make me wait any longer, damn you."

He pulled her against him, his body hot and ready. "That's what I like. Sweet talk."

She groaned, stroking his manhood. "Can't you remember what to do next?"

"I'm thinking." He brushed her between the legs, and she gasped.

"You're cruel, you know."

He sat up, and she grew frightened. "I didn't mean it. Don't go."

He stilled to look down at her, and with a wry grin he shook his head. "No man would leave you now, sweetheart. No sane man." He turned away, and after a few seconds she realized what he was doing.

"Oh..." She lay back on the bedroll, her emotions mixed. She wasn't insane, either, and there was no way she was leaving now. But it did bother her that he had condoms with him out here in the woods. "You're always ready, aren't you?" she said, surprised none of her frustration over that discovery made it into her tone.

He turned back. "Even if I did have a death wish, I wouldn't expect my partners to."

She stared into his handsome face. He wasn't grinning, but it wouldn't have made any difference as far as her sexual availability to him was concerned. Not at that moment, anyway. She was so high from his lovemaking, his sexy grin would have been downright redundant. Lifting her arms to encircle his neck, she forced all other thought from her mind. "I want to fly, now," she coaxed.

"I'm your man, sweetheart." He lifted himself over her, and she held her breath with anticipation. She felt the man-heat of him touch her between her thighs, and exaltation parted her lips. "Now..." she cried softly. "I need you now."

He closed his eyes, as though in prayer, then moved his hips, beginning a gentle stroking. There was nothing raw or rough about his lovemaking. Nothing hasty. She watched, wide-eyed, as he held the fantastic power of his body in solid check, drawing from her every vestige of sanity as he slowly, steadily, increased the pace of his movements.

Her breathing was coming in labored pants, her body wrapped in a glow of his tender, almost reverent ministrations. She clutched at his upper arms, rock-hard muscle beneath warm flesh.

As he increased the tempo, she grabbed at his shoulders, then raked her hands across his passion-slickened back, to cup his tense buttocks, to press him down, force him to take her fully. She whimpered, lolling her head from side to side, her body bubbling at a feverish pitch. She arched to meet him again and again, the rhythm of their lovemaking reverberating in her breast.

He was a master of the craft, for with each deepening thrust, he sent the fires of her need raging further and further out of control. She heard herself crying out over and over as she discovered such joy, such rapture, as she'd never known possible. She sounded so strange to her own ears, like some feral creature of the night, caught in a wily hunter's lethal snare.

She clutched at him, dug with her fingernails, as he brought her to the brink. She prayed the glorious sensations would never end, but sensed that no human being could survive such extreme physical pleasure for long.

The final, exquisite explosion of feeling began deep inside her, catapulting her past raw desire to utter fulfillment. In a pure, undisciplined burst of joy, she lifted herself completely away from the bedroll, sobbing out his name.

When, at last, she fell back to earth, he held her close, kissing her tearstained cheeks, murmuring endearments as she shuddered out her climax.

He jerked inside her, and she knew he'd also found release. "Stay with me tonight, Lorna," he whispered, his voice rough.

She lay in his embrace, drained and sated in a way she'd never known, not even with Bill. But with his throaty request, her chest tightened with a new, heady longing for him. Even the soft way he said her name turned her on. *Already?* Unable to believe herself, she could only nod, kissing him, relishing their intimate connection.

One night. That was what she'd meant when she made the promise to herself that it would only be once. She'd meant *only one night*.

Hadn't she?

7

Lorna lay in a tangle of arms and legs. A delicious, sensuous tangle. She was trapped, but she didn't feel trapped at all. She felt wonderful. At least her body felt wonderful. Her thoughts were anything but.

The first golden brush of dawn was beginning to light the sky. She closed her eyes and hugged the man who slept beside her, nestling her against his chest. She didn't want the night to end, and she had hardly slept, trying to savor every moment. She knew she was being stupid, holding the experience so tenderly in her heart, but she could no longer argue the fact that she was a compete fool where this man was concerned.

She'd been attracted to Clint from the first moment she saw him, and she'd fought it with all her heart and soul. Yet here she was, naked, her breasts crushed against his chest, his leg slung across hers, his arms cradling her gently, almost possessively.

He'd proved to be a better lover than Bill had been. She'd never thought that was possible, and she smiled wanly. Relishing the feel of his heartbeat as it thrummed through her, she touched his chest with what she could only have described as reverence. Toying with a tuft of chest hair, she damned herself for acquiring that knowledge about his sexual expertise. Stupid, indecisive idiot that she was.

Once again, her emotions had drawn her far afield from her goals. This was no safe, ordinary man. This man risked his life on a daily basis, for heaven's sake. If she had any brains at all, they wouldn't be worth what the search party would have to be paid to look for them.

He stirred, and it startled her when he captured the hand she had pressed to his chest and drew it to his lips, kissing her fingertips. "Morning," he said, drowsily. "Nice way to wake up."

She could detect his immediate arousal, and sucked in a startled breath. This couldn't be happening. Didn't he know it was over? The night was fading. It was a new day, a new reality. She couldn't let this go on. *"No..."* Pulling her hand from his, she struggled out of the bedroll, the chill of the morning on her nakedness making her shiver.

He came up on one elbow, looking tousled and sleepy and dangerously irresistible. "Was it something I said?" He took her ankle in his fingers, massaging with his thumb.

She grew weak, damp with renewed longing, but yanked away from his touch. "I said *once...*"

He grinned at her, his eyes shining with soft ardor. "You lied, sweetheart. I counted."

"Don't do this. You promised, too."

He sat up, the bedroll falling away from his chest. "Lorna. Don't go." No longer smiling, he took her hand. There was pain in the contact. But the pain was in her heart.

"I'm going." She jerked away. "We've gotten each other out of our systems, so we can move on." Grabbing her dress, she threw it on over her head to cover herself.

His expression skeptical, he watched her frantic activity.

"So you use me and then kick me to the curb?"

"That's not funny." She tugged on a boot.

"I'm not laughing." He'd spoken so softly, she stopped in the middle of yanking on her other boot to peer at him. His mercurial black eyes were narrowed. His jaw worked.

"Oh, please," she said, scoffing. "Just leave it be." Lurching to stand, she gathered up her underwear and socks, wadding them nervously in her hands.

"That's very romantic." His tone was mocking. "But before I...leave it be... I think you should know you're not out of *my* system, and I don't think I'm out of yours."

She'd spun away, but the insight halted her, and she remained absolutely motionless for an instant. Her lips trembled, and to quell it, she drew them between her teeth. *Lord, he was right. She didn't know if she could ever get him out of her system after...after...*

A galvanizing shudder ran through her at the memory of the beauty they'd shared during the night. But she couldn't admit it. Didn't dare allow any softening, or she knew it would happen between them again—and again. All too soon, she'd be hopelessly in love with another daredevil. A man she might suddenly, tragically, lose. She didn't think her heart could stand it again, and she would never put Sam through such torture.

At last, squaring her shoulders, she shook her head. "I—I've never known a man so *completely* out of my system as you are." The falsehood tasted bitter on her tongue as she stumbled away from him into the dawn.

Clint watched her go. Though his body ached to, he refused to follow her, to draw her down onto the grass and prove that she was lying through those sexy lips. He understood it was best that she go. It would have been even better if she'd taken her walk in another direction last night, or if he'd stayed on that damned bedroll and let her escape after she finished her nervous little llama speech.

But he'd been so astonished to see her there—right out of his fantasy—he'd ignored the bothersome voice in his head chiding him that he'd sworn *not* to get involved with her. *Damn his hide.*

He dragged both hands through his hair, cursing the gods for the fiendish tricks they played on mortals. Of all the places in the world to end up making love to Lorna Willow, he'd never have guessed it would be on this bedroll in this scrawny patch of trees. What had possessed him to bed down out here? Why hadn't he simply slept in the hangar?

As the golden morning stretched her fingers into the glade, his glance fell to his wrists, covered with crescent-shaped gouges and long scratches. He sucked in a deep breath at the sight of the physical imprint of Lorna's passions, and knew she'd left her mark on his back, too. She'd been an uninhibited kitten in bed, and the intensity of her ardor had made him do things he hadn't even known he could do.

He closed his eyes, experiencing a resurgence of desire for her. With a low groan, he lay back against the rough bark, almost relishing the pain the contact caused his scraped flesh. Damn him to hell, he deserved it for breaking his own rule about touching the woman.

He had a nagging suspicion that even after the scratches healed, he would still find himself recalling last night—for God knew how long.

Lorna was so tired she could hardly see straight, and she was starving. She knew she'd been cowardly to skip lunch at the diner with Reva and the other girls, but she'd been afraid Bo and Clint might show up. They seemed to make it in most days. And she had no intention of sharing anything as intimate as a lunch table with Clint McCord after last night!

She checked her watch. Just two o'clock? Good grief. How was she going to make it till five without falling asleep with her head in somebody's toilet? At least her next appointment was with a widow lady who lived alone. No lecherous bachelors would be lurking around to suggest that they test out the new shower head—together.

As she drove up before Mrs. Pullman's old Victorian house, she was shocked to see the white-haired octogenarian running toward the truck, waving a scarf. "Oh! Oh, Mrs. Willow!" she wheezed, clutching her throat and motioning anxiously toward her roof. "It's Mr. Bullock! He's stuck in my chimney!"

Lorna climbed down from the cab, following the frantic woman's gestures with a worried gaze. "You've got a man stuck in your chimney? I don't see—"

"No—no!" She grabbed hold of Lorna's arm with agitated, arthritic fingers. "He's my darling-boy cat. Mr. Bullock is fifteen years old, and he's just howling something fierce. I can hear him all over the house. You have a ladder, dear. You must save him."

Lorna looked at the steeply pitched roof. Even from her vantage point far below, she could see that there were loose wood shingles scattered about. She hated loosened shingles on a steeply pitched roof. They made working up there so treacherous. Though there were times when she had to climb on a roof to snake out pipes, she didn't like it. Heights weren't her favorite thing.

"Oh, my dear. Can you hear him? That's Mr. Bullock screaming."

Lorna could hear it now. The high-pitched yowling of a very frightened cat. "Oh, dear..." She couldn't stand to think of an animal suffering. "Okay, Mrs. Pullman. I'll get my ladder." It was against her better judgment, but she had to do what she could. Looking up at the chimney, which seemed almost in the clouds, she murmured, "Hold on, Mr. Bullock."

"Thank you, dear. I don't know what I would do if anything happened to my darling boy." The woman clutched her breast with her scarf-wielding hand. "You're a godsend."

Lorna nodded weakly, heading back to get her extension ladder. "Or, put another way," she mumbled, "I'm a sucker for animals."

Before she'd gotten the ladder set up, people had begun to come out of nearby houses, apparently having heard Mrs. Pullman's cries. Women, toddlers and elderly men stared at Lorna as though she were part of a circus act. They drew nearer as she climbed. Once she'd reached the roof, she looked back. Even a few cars were stopping. She supposed a cornflower-blue fire truck and a woman climbing on a house would be rather unusual sights in a small West Texas town. It occurred to her as she scrambled onto the slippery shingles that at least one of the onlookers might offer to *help*. Maybe all the gallant heroes in town were at the backhoe plant at this hour.

She stood, sucking in a breath as she got her balance. Then she slowly sidestepped up the slope. Her hands began to tingle, and so did her feet. Even when she went to movies in which people were on trapezes or scrambling over the tops of buildings making getaways, her hands and feet tingled from her fear of being in high places.

She tried to ignore her pounding heart and headed for the apex of the roof. Once she reached it, there was a burst of applause from below. She straddled the rim, which was lucky, for a shingle came loose, and she slipped, falling to her knees.

Someone on the ground screamed, and there were moans and groans. But when she caught herself, there was more applause. She refused to look down, fearful that she'd get sick to her stomach. She wondered how much applause there would be if she upchucked all over them.

"Kitty?" she called feebly, inching along the roof's peak on all fours. "Mr. Bullock? Are you okay?"

She heard a plaintive yowl and was relieved. At least he hadn't fallen

Once she reached the brick chimney, she pulled herself up and leaned over to have a look. The bricks inside had been set crookedly, with big globs of mortar sticking out. Some of the bricks were cracked and loose. The chimney didn't appear all that sturdy. "Mr. Bullock?" she called, not seeing anything but darkness in the grimy cavity.

There was a mournful meow, and she bent farther over, catching sight of the swish of a dark tail. "Good boy." Reaching down, she felt around the ashy walls. "Now don't be scared. Come to Auntie Lorna."

The cat meowed again, and it sounded very much like "Help me." She strained, stretching as far as she could, and was rewarded by the brush of fur against her fingertips, but she couldn't quite reach him. He was under a big glob of mortar, perched on a crooked outcropping of brick.

Knowing she was being foolhardy, she lifted her foot and found an indentation in the exterior of the chimney. Boosting herself farther over, she grabbed the other side for support and lowered her head deeper into the pit. "Mr. Bullock?" She choked, not only from the soot but from the pressure of the chimney bricks on her stomach. Blood was rushing to her head, and her nausea was getting worse.

She had to straighten up. When she did, she gulped in fresh air and threw a leg over to straddle the chimney wall. Bits of loose mortar fell away into the chasm. When she didn't feel quite as sick, she leaned in, grasping the other side of the chimney. Poor, frightened Mr. Bullock was on his hind legs, stretching toward her. His yellow eyes and his two white forepaws were all that was clearly visible.

"Oh, good, you trust me." She gingerly edged down until she only had a knee slung across the chimney wall. Her other boot had found a foothold in the rough, sooty surface, and she was able to reach far enough to grasp the animal by the loose skin at his neck, then tow him up.

As soon as she did, he scrambled to her neck and held on for dear life, making good use of his claws. She winced, but tried to ignore it as she slowly pulled them both out of the black hole.

Once she was straddling the chimney again, with Mr. Bullock wrapped securely around her neck, the crowd below hooted and clapped. She patted the cat and spoke soothingly to it. "I don't know why they're clapping. Do you? We're not down yet."

She slid off the chimney to set her boots on the peak of the roof. Once there, she straddled it again, sitting down, her limbs too shaky for her to go anywhere for a while. It took all her strength just to peel the frightened animal from her shoulders. Settling it in her lap, she crooned to it, stroking its sleek back as it tried to climb back up to her throat. "Settle down, Mr. Bullock, we may be here for a while."

"You're nuts, you know."

She blinked at the cat, startled that its meows were starting to sound very human—even familiar. Or was she just too light-headed from lack of sleep and food to trust her wits?

She noticed movement where the ladder was. A man was climbing onto the roof—a man with dark, unruly hair and tremendously wide shoulders. She could never again mistake those shoulders and that hair. She'd known them too intimately. "Clint?" Her racing heart upped its tempo. "What are you doing here?"

He stood up and began to make his way carefully toward her. "Let's just say I love sideshows."

She blanched, clutching the now purring cat to her breasts. "You shouldn't be here."

He made it all the way without mishap and sat down beside her. "Give me the cat."

"He's fine with me. He's purring."

"Dammit. I saw you almost fall on your way up here. That cat won't be purring when you tumble head over heels to the ground with it."

She lifted a mutinous chin. "What are you, the roof patrol?" Why did it have to be Clint who'd come to her rescue? Any other man who'd ventured up here to help would have been welcomed with a huge smile and probably a hug. But not Clint. She'd already been in his arms once today, and she didn't plan to let it happen again, not ever—not even in gratitude. "I climb on roofs all the time in my work," she retorted. Unable to cope with his nearness one second longer, she stood and started to pick her way down the sheer slope, stubbornly clutching Mr. Bullock to her breast.

"All right. Have it your way." She felt a grip on her arm. "Crazy woman."

She skidded on another loose shingle, and his grasp kept her from losing her balance. A collective gasp rose from the gathering on the lawn as she steadied herself. Taking a restorative breath, she peered at him, her eyes glistening with grudging thanks.

With a nod, he indicated that she should go on. He said nothing all the way to the ground, where Mrs. Pullman rushed up and whisked her cat away, sobbing happily into its fur.

Lorna breathed a sigh of relief. As she rubbed her damp, grimy hands on her streaked overalls, some of the spectators came over and spoke to her and patted her back. Smiling tiredly, she happened to notice out of the corner of her eye that Clint was taking down her ladder. She hurried to him, grabbing at it. "I can do that."

He didn't let go, just hefted it under one arm and tromped off toward the truck. Fairly sure a wrestling match on Mrs. Pullman's lawn would really turn this thing into a sideshow, she just followed him, grabbing one end of the ladder. After they lifted it up on its hooks, she turned toward the cab to retrieve her toolbox, but Clint blocked her way. Concern etched his features.

"Look." She sighed audibly. "Thanks for your help. But I have a leaky water heater to fix."

She tried to brush past him, but he caught her arm. "And you think *I'm* reckless?"

She jerked against his hold, but he wouldn't release her. "You're making too much out of it. I wouldn't have fallen. I'm just a little tired—"

"What if I were you and you were Sam? What if he'd been up there?"

Her eyes widened at the horrible thought. She would have been furious at her son if he'd done anything that half-witted. But who was Clint—Mr. Daredevil—McCord to tell her how to live her life? Angry, she yanked free. "I'm an adult, so—"

"So you should know better."

That did it! How dare he! "Don't you talk to me about knowing better! You have no right to reprimand me about *anything!* You risk your life crash-diving your plane every weekend!"

His eyes were black as pitch, intense and direct. "Dammit, I don't—" His nostrils flaring, he cut himself off and slouched back against the cab door. "Forget it. You're right." He crossed his arms before his chest, looking frustrated. "Your life is none of my business."

Something on his arms caught her attention, and without thinking, she reached out, touching a gash. "What happened to you?"

He seemed to jerk at her touch, or did she imagine it? Her glance lifted to his face. "You have a short memory, sweetheart," he said gruffly.

It hit her suddenly and hard what those scratches meant, and just when he'd received them. "Oh...my...Lord..." she breathed. "Did I do that?"

He chuckled, but there was little humor in it. "Maybe I do live dangerously, after all." She felt something brush her cheek, and stepped back to a safe distance.

"Your face is dirty, Mrs. Willow." He held out his handkerchief, smudged with soot. "Think of it as a loan. From your landlord."

Absently she took the proffered kerchief. Clearly, he wanted the subject changed, and she decided it was a good idea. "Thanks..." Her glance drifted to his injuries, and her cheeks burned with shame. She must have lost her mind last night.

"I meant to tell you." He hooked a finger along the bib of her overalls, tugging lightly before he dropped his hand. "You shouldn't, either."

She stopped wiping her cheek, confused. "I shouldn't, either—what?"

"Wear clothes. It's a crime." He grinned at her, but there was no sign of it in his eyes.

Lorna didn't have a date. Well, she did, but she begged off, moving it to next week. She was too tired. If the truth were told, she was simply not in the mood. She'd had a very long night, and an unnerving day, and all she wanted to do was visit with her son and get to bed early.

It was just as well, since Sam had no one to baby-sit for him, anyway. Bo and Maggie had offered to take him along on their picnic, but Lorna didn't think that allowing a young boy to tag along on a lovers' moonlit outing would be very wise.

And, naturally, Clint had a date.

She'd showered and put on jeans and a T-shirt. Then she and Sam whipped up a quick and simple Spanish-rice recipe that he'd learned in 4-H camp. The meal was surprisingly tasty. They laughed and talked and tried to play Monopoly. But Barney insisted on dashing across the board, scattering hotels willy-nilly. And when he was reprimanded, he retaliated by shredding the play money. Even so, it was a great evening—as long as she kept her mind off a certain pilot and his "dinner" companion not far away.

"Time for bed, honey." She gathered up the money that was still worth keeping and stacked it. "Better get into your pajamas."

"Okay, Mom."

She placed the game board in its box and put on the lid, yawning. It was only nine, but she was pooped.

"*Mom!*" Sam said the word so sharply she jerked around in sudden fright.

"What's wrong?"

"It's Aunt Bee. She's not here!"

"Did she get out of her cage?"

"No," he cried, his face puckered in distress. "I forgot and left her in Clint's office this afternoon." He smacked his forehead. "Stupid! Stupid! Stupid!"

Lorna leaned against the card table, relieved. "Oh, honey, you scared me to death. It's no tragedy. She'll be fine until tomorrow."

He looked stricken. "Oh—but Aunt Bee can't sleep without me. Please!"

"But Mr. McCord has company."

"Not in his office. And Aunt Bee was almost out of water, Mom."

She felt a surge of defeat. "Well . . . go on over and get her, then. Just don't bother—"

"Thanks!" He spun toward the door, then turned back. "Wanna come?"

She was surprised by the invitation, and probably showed it. "Don't you think you can make it alone?"

He shrugged. "Yeah, but I know you like to take walks."

She shook her head, leaning heavily on the table, her mind riveted on what had happened the last time she took a walk around here. "Thanks, honey, but not tonight. And remember—Mr. McCord has company."

"Okay."

When he disappeared, she took in a deep gulp of air, surprised she'd been holding her breath. The very idea of seeing Clint with another woman made her heart contract painfully. Forcing the thought back, she picked up the game and took it into her bedroom to replace it in the cardboard box under her bed. After she'd stored it, she sat down on the bed and covered her face with her hands. Why couldn't she be crazy about canasta or dried frogs?

"Mom!" came Sam's mournful shout. *"Mom!"*

She'd just begun to slip out of her jeans when he yelled, so she yanked them back up and ran into the living room to find her son bouncing around in agitation, his features anguished. An empty cage was dangling in his hand, its door gaping. "Aunt Bee's lost!" he cried. "Do you think she's dead?"

Lorna hurried to her son and knelt to look at the cage. The door latch was broken. She grimaced. How many times had she noticed that the wire was cracked? How many times had she promised herself she'd fix it? And now? "Oh, honey." She hugged his shoulders. "Where was the cage?"

"In Clint's office, like I said." His voice broke. "If she got outside, something might have eaten her."

"I doubt that's what happened." She squeezed his shoulders to reassure him. "She's probably hiding right in the office." Though she was sick to her stomach about what she had to do, she stood, prying the cage from his clenched fist. "Let's go over and look. What did Mr. McCord say?"

"I didn't bother him, like you said."

That was the best news she'd had all day. "Oh—well, fine. Let's go, then."

He ran the back of his hand across his nose and sniffed, looking slightly mollified by her words. "Thanks." Spinning around, he ran out the door and was halfway back before she worked up her nerve to leave the cottage. What was it about distressed animals today? And why did they have to keep bringing her into dangerously close proximity with Clint McCord? She only hoped Aunt Bee would come rolling out from under a desk and toddle over to Sam before she got there.

Lorna had never been in Clint's office. The front door of the building opened onto a hallway that paralleled the entrance. So there was hardly anything to see as you entered, except a wall with a door off to the left and another on the right. She knew his apartment was one way and his office the other, but she didn't know which was which, and had decided it was best to remain totally ignorant.

Apparently Clint was a trusting soul, for the front door was unlocked. Or maybe he'd left it open for Bo. Whichever, when she arrived, Sam was nowhere to be seen. Though there were lights on in the left side of the building, more lights had just blinked on in the right side of the downstairs. Apparently that was the office, and that was where she'd find her son.

"Sam?" she ventured. The door to the right was open, so she went that way. "Sam?"

"Yeah, Mom?" His blond head popped up from behind a big wooden desk that held a computer, a phone and a stack of papers. Behind the desk was a glass-fronted trophy case, brimming with gold and silver cups and medals. Some were big and looked quite impressive. She supposed she shouldn't be surprised that he was very good at flying—too.

She surveyed the utilitarian room. The floor was shiny oak planks, the walls painted off-white. Fluorescent lighting made the place seem a little eerie at night.

The back wall was lined with bulletin boards, maps and charts. At the front, under the windows, a long counter housed a fax machine, a small copier and a two-way radio. Beneath that, the wall was completely covered by built-in files and cabinets. She had to admit she was impressed. She'd thought his workplace would be the chaos of a thrill-seeking lunatic. At least he was a well-organized, tidy lunatic.

At the other end of the room sat a large wooden box, standing nearly five feet tall and about the size of a kitchen table. She had no idea what it held. Maybe he'd just received a new plane engine by mail, or a set of tires. Possibly a week's supply of condoms. She bit her lip. *Where had that thought come from?*

Something caught her eye near the door. A framed poem. Stepping over to it, she scanned the verse. It spoke of a breed of men who couldn't settle down in one place for long, who roamed the world at will—of men who broke hearts at every turn in their solitary journey. These reckless, independent spirits found their God, their family and their true love in one simple word—*freedom.*

She looked away hastily from the revealing poem. Her vision blurry, she blinked back tears. That certainly said it all. Clint's Code—breaking hearts and moving on. Well, at least he was up-front about it. He even emblazoned it right there in his office, to make sure women didn't get confused and try to cling to him when it was over. Luckily, she had no intention of clinging.

"Aunt Bee?" Sam called. "Come on out, Aunt Bee. Don't be scared."

She heard the worry in his voice, and realized she needed to get her mind on her business and off Clint McCord. With the practiced eye of a mother who'd found many a wayward action figure over the years, she scanned the office for likely hedgehog hiding places. One leaped immediately into her view. The farthest lower counter door was slightly ajar. She walked over to it and opened it further, kneeling to peer inside.

There were hardbound ledgers, colorful folders, all neatly lined up on two shelves. The bottom shelf, a scant two inches from the floor, had a small space at one side where nothing was stored. Just the right size for a burrowing, frightened hedgehog to curl up in and await her young, tow-headed savior. And there she was. Lorna

smiled with relief. "Okay, Aunt Bee. Let's go home."
Grasping the spiky ball, she lifted her head. "I found her,
Sam. She's okay."

The skitter of feet told her he was racing over. She
turned, smiling, handing the boy his recovered pet. "I'm
sorry about the door latch. I'll fix it tonight."

Sam cuddled Aunt Bee to his cheek. "Thanks, Mom.
You're great." He was grinning with contentment. His
cheeks were bright pink from anxiety, and she was sorry
her procrastination had put him through this. "I'm taking her back. Okay?"

"Sure." When she pushed herself to her feet, she was
appalled to notice a tall figure lounging at the office entrance.

"Oh, hi, Clint," Sam called cheerfully. "I lost Aunt
Bee."

He nodded toward Lorna. "I know. I saw Kojak over
there find her."

Now it was Lorna's turn to have pink cheeks. She didn't
know why she was blushing, but for whatever reason, her
face felt inordinately warm. Could it be because he was
wearing a white dress shirt and slacks, and it was patently
obvious their presence had interrupted his entertaining?

She'd never seen him dressed up, and she felt strangely
sick at heart that he'd gone to so much trouble. Who was
this special woman? Why did she have the errant hope that
he'd chosen to wear long sleeves merely to hide the
scratches? Balling her hands, she castigated herself for
caring. Yet, even as she did, her glance roved on to note
that he didn't have on a tie, but he was wearing shoes.
Apparently they hadn't interrupted too much. She wondered if that would have still been true in another hour.

"Hi." He casually crossed his legs at his ankles, looking so carelessly handsome it hurt.

"Hello," she murmured thickly. "We were just..."

"I know," he said.

"Well, I gotta get to bed," Sam said. "Say, Clint. Why don't you show Mom your stimulator. She'd love it."

Clint's eyebrows dipped for the briefest second; then he grinned at the boy. "If she wants to see it." His glance drifted to her.

"She'll get excited."

With that, Sam was gone, leaving the two to stare at each other across a deafening silence.

"Out of the mouths of babes," he said at last, his dark gaze murky with some emotion she couldn't quite define.

Her eyes had gone wide and were prickly-dry, but his low taunt brought her back. She blinked, working to keep her poise. "I—I don't even want to know." As she edged toward the door, she cleared her throat to erase the tremor from her voice. "Show it to your dinner guest."

"She's seen ... *it*."

Lorna experienced a sinking despair, but made her face a nonchalant mask. "Why doesn't *it* surprise me?" When she reached the door, he didn't move out of her way, but he wasn't quite blocking her, either. Avoiding eye contact, she muttered, "I'll get the lights."

"Have a ball."

His cologne assailed her with unwanted memories, and she missed the switch the first time she reached for it.

"Need help?"

She shook her head, managed to flip the switch, then realized her mistake. She was in the dark with Clint McCord. Staring past him toward the moonlit entry, she said stiffly, "Sorry about interrupting you."

"Lorna. Look at me." He lifted a hand, placing it on the other doorjamb, effectively blocking her exit. "Please."

She blanched. There was a shallowness to her breath and a tight ache growing in her stomach. She wanted so badly for him to take her into his arms, make love to her right there, but she knew that was crazy thinking. She told her legs to break past him, to duck and run, but somehow she couldn't obey her own commands. After only a brief hesitation, his soft request won out. "What?" she whispered.

In the dim light she could see the glint of teeth flash in a brief grin. "It's a *simulator*, sweetheart." He'd spoken in a neutral voice, but she sensed annoyance—and something else. He indicated the office with a nod. "That big box over there is a flight simulator. Don't get paranoid that I've been showing your son lewd sex toys."

Astonished by his quiet revelation, she glanced over her shoulder to stare at the box. A shaft of moonglow highlighted it. *Of course.* A flight simulator! What else could it have been? She felt like such an idiot for picturing some sort of Barbarella sex machine. "Oh, dear— Maybe I—"

"Maybe," he said, interrupting her. "Good night, Mrs. Willow."

When she turned around, he was gone.

8

It seemed like old home week in the Brazen Gulch Hotel's restaurant. Everyone in town that Lorna knew was there. Reva was huddled with—of all people—the toe-sucker. When she spotted Lorna, she shrugged sheepishly and waved. Apparently she hadn't been as disgusted by Herm-the-foot-fetishist as she pretended.

Bo and Maggie were there, too. They were holding hands at a dark corner table, with eyes only for each other. Even Thelma was in attendance. Somehow Lorna wasn't surprised to see the shy librarian with Clyde Canasta—er, Simmons. She had a feeling Thelma and Clyde would spend their twilight years together, blissful in their mutual love of canasta. And when they died, somebody would have to pry playing cards from their fingers.

The restaurant was darkly lit and had a remarkably authentic Olde-English atmosphere. Classical music was piped in, and every table held a flickering candle. The place was jammed, even though it was a Monday night. The only person she didn't see was Clint McCord. Thank heaven. She'd avoided him for a solid week, but that didn't mean she'd managed to keep thoughts of him from messing up her mind.

Tamping down troubling memories, she forced a smile and nodded at Norbert's comment about Dostoyevski, and how the novelist had held the Russian poet Pushkin in the highest regard. Norbert had a long, thin, friendly face, and could have been considered handsome, unless you insisted on a chin.

Most of the evening, his heavy eyebrows had been drawn down in scholastic concentration, and he'd only smiled when the food came. He said something else about Dostoyevski's works, how they were dotted with Pushkin quotes, but she was working so hard at not crossing her eyes with boredom, she wasn't catching the whole drift.

"Most so-called authorities say Pushkin was a liberal," he was saying as he took a large bite of his lasagna. With his mouth stuffed, he went on, "Oh, they yammer about how he defended Russia's suppression of a Polish uprising in 1830, but as far as I'm concerned, that's bunk. Don't you agree, Lorna?"

Caught off guard, she tried to focus, not having expected him to actually address her after thirty minutes of nonstop lecturing. Taking a stalling sip of coffee, she swallowed. "Well, Norbert, to be honest, I don't know that much about either Dostoyevski or Pushkin." She smiled apologetically as he absorbed this grievous news. She could tell that he was absorbing it and that it was grievous, because he'd completely stopped eating—another thing he hadn't stopped doing in the past thirty minutes.

Frowning, he took another bite, then leaned toward her. "You *are* kidding, aren't you?"

She shook her head; this time her smile was real. How could the man be so one-tracked? Since he was personnel director of the Brazen Backhoe Company, she wondered if all his applicants for employment were grilled on their knowledge of Russian humanities. "I'm afraid the subject doesn't come up much in my line of work."

"But—but in your free time, surely you read!"

She shrugged. "Oddly, not that much Russian literature."

"What about *Crime and Punishment, The Idiot* and *The Possessed?*"

She grimaced, but playfully. "Screwed-up priorities?"

He wiped his mouth with his napkin. His wrinkled forehead told her he didn't realize she was joking. "Well, I'll loan you those three. Next week we can talk about them."

She allowed her glance to drop to her plate of cooling spaghetti. How was she going to tell this guy there wouldn't be a next week? Not with him, anyway. "Well, er, will you excuse me a minute? I'd like to powder my nose." Before he could respond, she'd scooped up her purse and stood. When she turned to go, she slammed head-on into a solid human wall. The shock of the contact made her stumble.

If powerful arms hadn't come around her, she would have fallen. She grabbed for dear life, clasping a very sturdy man around a marvelously male chest. Though he staggered a step back in surprise, thankfully, their impact hadn't unbalanced him.

"Whoa." There was a male chuckle as strong arms pulled her close. "I didn't know this was our dance."

Recognition hit with the familiar voice and scent, and a shiver of hysteria raced through her. It was Clint. Of all people to crash into. Her cheek was nestled against his warm white dress shirt, and her arms were squeezing him around his sport jacket. She tried to block out the imp in her brain that was taunting, "He smells *so* sexy." It was impossible to keep her pulse from beating wildly, and almost as impossible to give him up now that she was holding him again.

"Are you okay?" His lips brushed her forehead.

She nodded, easing herself backward. "I—I'm fine." Her stomach was clenched, her pulse erratic, but she tried to keep her voice calm.

He let her go, too, his hands lingering only a second longer than necessary. She knew she had to look him in the eye to apologize, and apprehension made her wince as she made the effort. "I'm sorry—" His smile was as intimate as a kiss, and as debilitating. She lost her voice.

"Hi." His glance swept over her approvingly, then shifted to take in her date. His grin didn't waver. "How's it going?"

She examined the pretty woman behind him. Apparently he'd been about to help her take her seat at a nearby table. She was blond and beautiful and clearly annoyed that his attention had been diverted. Trying to regain her wits, she dragged her eyes from the woman's pretty pout. "Uh, Mr. McCord, do you know Norbert Sex?" She skimmed his chin with her glance in order to avoid direct eye contact, indicating her date with a gesture.

"Really?" He chuckled. "That must be a hell of a conversation starter."

She looked at Clint, confused. His gaze was softly teasing.

Norbert put down his fork and stood. "I'm sure she meant to say *Stepp*."

"What did I say?" she asked as the men clasped hands.

"You said *sex*, Lorna dear," Norbert explained in the same scholarly tone he'd used all evening. "Who knows why?"

"Freud may know," Clint murmured loud enough for only her to hear. He held eye contact with her just long enough to see her grasp her blunder. When her eyes had gone wide, he turned back to her date, his grin crooked.

"Nice to meet you, Stepp. I'm Clint McCord." He let go of the man's hand, then dropped a casual arm about the blonde's shoulders. "Connie Blanchard, meet my tenant, Mrs. Lorna Willow, and her friend, Norbert Stepp."

The woman reached up and entwined her fingers with Clint's. "Lovely to meet y'all. I'm visitin' from Houston."

The humiliation from her slip of the tongue was bad enough, but adding the discomfort of watching Clint and his blond friend together made her want to scream. She couldn't stand it one more second. She mumbled something she hoped sounded polite and *didn't* contain the word *sex,* and practically ran to the ladies' room.

Once she was alone, she glared in the gilded mirror and called herself all the names she deserved to be called—*Idiot! Jellyfish! Fool!* Somewhere in the middle of her tirade, she heard a sob in her voice and stopped dead. Though her image blurred before her, it was suddenly horribly clear that she must add an adjective to that stack of distasteful nouns.

She bit her lip and it throbbed like her pulse. The adjective was *jealous.*

Lorna wanted a nice, safe man, so why was she standing at Clint's door in the middle of the night, prepared to knock? She'd even barged inside the front entry and was lurking at his apartment door. *Let her libido rot in hell for this betrayal!*

She knew he was in there alone, because she'd seen him come back by himself from his date with the blonde. That had been hours ago. Enough hours for her to go completely insane, it appeared. Even after tossing and turning, then pacing as she counseled with herself about how wrong he was for her, she was still here at his door, her fist raised and ready.

She moved her forearm to knock, but her knuckles wouldn't quite meet the wood. Sighing aloud, she tried again. Still her hand made no contact. It was as though some tiny vestige of sanity remained, trying valiantly to keep her on the straight and narrow pathway toward her goal.

She pulled her lips between her teeth, irresolute. Wanting to stay, needing to go. She just stood there with one clenched fist raised, looking like a statue glorifying some kind of power— "Power to the Cowards," maybe?

She managed to take a hard-fought step backward, trying to break free of the outlandish, dreamlike lunacy of it all. Her mind shrieked at her to turn and bolt toward the cottage, but her legs remained rooted. All her years of fear about getting involved with another daredevil were still locked tight inside her heart, yet her heart seemed to be set on this daredevil. What kind of dimwit did that make her?

She managed another step away, and swallowed with trepidation. Her throat was so dry it hurt, but the bare beginning of her retreat was a good sign. She sucked in deep breaths. Actually, it sounded more like panting, as she worked to quell her heartbeat, which had been pounding out of control ever since she'd thrown on jeans and a T-shirt and started this mad trek.

The door was flung open, and Lorna almost died of a heart attack right there. Paralyzed with one fist still poised in the air, she gaped, not quite believing Clint was standing before her. He was clad in a pair of low-slung sweatpants, his belly and chest burnished in the moonlight. Dark eyebrows slanted in a frown as he watched her uncertainly. "Why the hell don't you knock?" he whispered huskily.

Her lips sagged open. "How— How—" She was so stunned, she couldn't get the question out. He looked so sexy and cuddly and—and *waiting?*

He took her hands, drawing her into his apartment. "I've been sitting here in the dark, wanting you," he admitted. "I don't believe in mental telepathy, but dammit, you're here, and you're not leaving."

All her mental chaos dissipated like mist at the first touch of sunshine, replaced by an upsurge of longing. She knew he didn't want to get married, knew he would eventually end their affair. But she couldn't seem to keep away from him. With a defeated whimper that sounded like a sigh in the night stillness, she threw her arms about his neck. "I *do* believe in mental telepathy, and I plan to blame this on you."

He chuckled, lifting her into his arms. "Go right ahead."

She had a horrible thought. "Where's Bo?"

"With Maggie, at her place." Even though it was dark and she'd never been in Clint's apartment before, she sensed she was being whisked through a living room, then down a hall. "Is Sam sleeping over somewhere?" he asked.

She snuggled in his embrace as they entered his bedroom. "Uh-huh."

He kissed the tip of her nose. "I like it when he sleeps over."

She held tighter to his neck, experiencing a surge of guilt. "I don't."

When her hips touched his mattress, he vowed softly, "You'll feel better about it in a minute."

His promise was sealed with a kiss, and Lorna felt much, much better very quickly. With touches that were light and almost painfully teasing, he short-circuited her senses as he lovingly removed her clothes. Drawing her closer, ever closer, to the brink of insanity, he made her writhe and cry out as he pleasured and satisfied her. Again and again, the arousing exploration of his hands and his lips made her quiver and claw, drawing from him answering groans of desire that moved them toward heightened explorations of wilder, more erotic play.

Much later, her body exhausted and tingling with release, she snuggled against him, grazing his chest with her lips. "You couldn't have had sex with your blonde tonight and still have this much energy."

"I didn't." He kissed the top of her head. "I'm not obsessed with her."

She smiled in the darkness, but tried to keep it out of her voice. "Oh? Who are you obsessed with, then?"

"Who?" he murmured, sounding dubious.

"Mmm-hmm."

He'd been lying on his back, but he propped himself on his side and looked down at her. "Sweetheart, do you honestly think I can keep up this pace with most women?"

She pursed her lips as though in thought. "Do you consider this pace tiring?"

He grinned, teasing her breast with his thumb. "I consider it debilitating."

She arched up to meet his touch, sighing. "Then—what are you doing now?"

He lowered his lips to the stimulated nub, kissing her there, then tormenting her with his clever tongue. "Hell if I know..."

She felt his arousal once again and slid her hand down to grasp him. His wonderful, rock-hard body taunted, tempted her into another wild surrender.

Lifting his lips from her breast, he asked, "What about you and Mr. Sex?"

She giggled. "Oh, yes, Norbert satisfied me right there on the restaurant table. Didn't you watch?"

He lifted his head to gaze at her, his expression solemn. "Yes, I did."

She blinked, startled by the grave tone in his voice. "You did?"

He grunted out a laugh. "You're the one who told me to go to hell, remember?"

She closed her eyes as another torrent of guilt rushed through her, but she was unable to release him. She stroked lovingly for a long moment, and it was only when he groaned that she looked at him.

"Make up your mind, sweetheart," he warned gruffly. "Are we going to make love or fight? I can't stand it much longer."

She didn't want to fight, least of all now. Managing a smile, she whispered, "Kiss me?"

His eyes held vague misgivings as he lowered his lips to hers.

Dawn again. *Damn.* Clint wondered why darkness always had to be followed by dawn. Who in blazes had made it a rule that night had to ceaselessly turn into day? Why couldn't they live in Alaska or Antarctica, where the nights were six months long? He instinctively knew the answer to that question. Because Lorna's lovemaking would kill him, that was why.

He laced his fingers behind his head and grinned at the ceiling, murmuring, "But, like they say, what a way to go."

Lorna moved and sighed, her fingers resting on his chest, twitching slightly. He looked down at the small, pale hand. She didn't really have long fingernails. Just potent ones. He covered her fingers with his, then held them. Long and slender. Cool skin.

Inhaling, he filled his lungs with the scent of her. He could only describe her scent as—what? Freshly baked pumpkin pie was all he could come up with. He grinned, amazed at how much he liked that fragrance in a woman. This one, especially. He could almost see her with a can of pie filling, rubbing the stuff at her pulse points.

With a sudden rush of desire, he lifted her hand to his lips, kissing her knuckle. Delicious.

"What are you doing?" she asked thickly as her eyes languidly opened, then closed, then opened a bit wider.

"I'm tasting you." He kissed again.

"Mmmmm." Her lashes fluttered closed.

He grinned at her. "Sleepy?"

"Mmmmm."

"Tired?"

"Mmmmm."

"Turned on?"

Her eyes came open. "Hmmm?"

"Would you like to be?" He drew three of her fingers into his mouth.

"Clint!" She was fully awake now.

"Hmmm?"

She struggled up on one elbow. "Clint, we can't."

"Oh, yes, we can. Or haven't you been paying attention?"

She yanked her hand from his sensual ministrations. "Maybe we'd better talk, now."

She scooted away, covering herself with the sheet. It was clear she was retreating emotionally again, and he felt the withdrawal like a boot in his gut. "What is it with you and daylight?" he muttered, sitting up. "You come to me in the dark, draw blood, then disappear. Sweetheart, I've seen that movie. I didn't like it much then, and I hate it now."

She looked abashed and cast a glance at her hands, clutching the sheet before her. "I—I'm sorry. It's just that I'm attracted to you."

"I don't consider that a bad thing."

"Clint . . ." She cast him a forlorn look. "Please."

His frown deepened. "Why don't I think this is foreplay?"

She exhaled aloud. "Look. You're not interested in marriage, right?"

He leaned tiredly against his headboard. "Right."

"I think for the kind of man you are, that's wise."

"I'm gratified we agree about one thing, anyway. But why should that stop us from finding pleasure in each other?"

She cast her glance away and frowned toward the window, where dawn was blossoming into day. "It's getting late."

"Oh, no, you don't." He sat forward and took her hand. "You're going to tell me why every morning after we've made love you decide you can't do it again."

She stiffened at his touch, but didn't fight him. Apparently she could sense his determination, and she allowed him to lower her hand to the bed and continue to hold her wrist. Even so, she refused to look at him. "I've been a widow for ten years, Clint. Sam's never known a father. I moved here because I decided it was time he had one, time I found a nice, normal man to share my life with. I didn't come here to have an affair with a nutcase who has a—"

"Death wish? I know, I've heard this speech before." He was so irritated he could hardly keep his voice calm. "What if I told you I don't have a death wish?"

She peered at him. "Sure you don't."

"What if I told you you're more reckless than I am?"

"Be serious." She looked away, this time yanking on his hold. "I have to go to work." She slid to the side of the bed, dropping one leg over the edge. His glance followed the movement to the pale, slender limb, so recently wrapped around his hips as they rode together to paradise. "Let go, Clint," she pleaded in a forlorn whisper.

He looked at her face. Her expression was one of mute wretchedness. Even in his anger and frustration, he couldn't refuse her. "I'll walk you to the door," he muttered, releasing his hold.

"No." She leaped up and started gathering her clothes.

"Don't be that way." He noticed her panties and picked them up. Refusing to make eye contact, she grabbed them and slipped them on. In a matter of seconds, she was dressed and dashing from his bedroom. A fragment of pink caught his eye, and he realized her bra was in the tangle of his sheets. Hooking a strap with a finger, he followed her out. "You forgot this."

She spun around and snatched it, her cheeks going crimson. Stuffing the bit of lace in her hip pocket, she muttered, "If I ever show up at your door again, throw a bucket of ice water on me."

The bang of his apartment door, then a second bang, told him she was beyond hearing any answer, even if it had been one she might care to hear. It wouldn't have been.

He walked to the same window through which he'd seen her coming last night and watched her run away from him. A strange dullness settled over his heart, and he clutched the windowsill. "Sweetheart, if you ever come to me again with soft desire in those big eyes, don't count on a bucket of water."

Lorna heard a knock at her door and groaned. She wasn't in any position for company—especially if the company was who she was afraid it was. She'd seen Clint several times during the past two weeks, either taking some clingy woman up in his plane or practicing one heart-in-the-throat stunt or another. And he'd had the nerve to suggest she was more reckless than he! The man was delusional. He also had terrible timing. She'd managed to avoid him for nearly half the month of August, so why was he coming by on her first free Friday afternoon?

"Can you get that, Udell?"

"Sure," her guest called from the living room.

She shifted, trying to get more comfortable. Why she'd offered to be involved in this project was beyond her. But the Boy Scout leader had needed a new drain pan on Tuesday, and he'd started talking about their project, and before she knew it, she'd volunteered to help. She shook her head at herself. She'd done lots of strange things for charity, but wearing a swimsuit and sitting in a bathtub filled with jelly beans was brand-new for her.

"It's your landlord with the mail," her male guest called.

"Just have him leave it on the table, Udell." She had a thought. "Oh, and bring me the bowling ball. We don't want to forget that!"

As footfalls approached, she wriggled to ease back against the rim of the tub to rest her head. Somehow Udell Maxwell, the school's math teacher, had miscalculated the number of beans they needed to order, and the scouts had had to make a quick run into Brazen Gulch for more. She only hoped there were enough in the small town. They would have to scour every place that might sell them, from the gas station to the movie theater. Udell estimated one more bucketful would top out the tub, and each bean had to be counted first. She longed for the boys to be back soon. She was starting to feel sticky.

There was a knock at the bathroom door.

"Come on in. It just blew shut in the breeze."

The door creaked open, and there stood Clint, a bowling ball in one hand and a stack of mail in the other. His dark eyes narrowed as he scanned her, sitting there, up to her neck in multicolored candy.

"Oh...." She clenched handfuls of beans beneath the surface, trying to hide her nervousness. "I—I thought you'd be Udell."

Incredulity rode his features as he hefted the bowling ball. "Where do you want this thing?" The question was asked through clenched jaws.

She indicated the foot of the tub. "Put it in down there, but be careful of my feet."

He lowered it into the jelly beans, not letting go until he'd settled it on the bottom. His hand grazed her inner calf, but she was so weighted down, she couldn't shift away. When he drew out his arm, he gave her another glance, annoyance hovering in his gaze. "Where do you want your mail, in the ice cream?"

His sarcasm irked her. "I asked you to leave it on the table."

He nodded. "Table. Check." He turned to go, then shifted back, the corner of his mouth twisting with aggravation. "This is your idea of a *normal* date?"

"There's a simple explanation—"

"Fine," he interjected as the bathroom door slammed at his back.

She sagged, closing her eyes, her calf still thrumming from the warm brush of his flesh.

An hour later the jelly bean count was complete, and the scouts and their leader were gone. Sam had asked to be excused from 4-H camp to help, saying that, after all, she was his mother. She'd relented. The kid hadn't even blinked an eye at his mother's latest adventure. She didn't know if that was a good or a bad thing. But she didn't see how she could be warping his psyche too badly by helping out the Boy Scouts—even if the "help" they'd asked for might be a touch bizarre.

Lorna showered, changed into shorts and a T-shirt and grabbed her toolbox. Since she'd given herself the afternoon off, she ambled over to the hangar where Sam had gone, after the jelly bean count, to help Bo.

Sam had told her Clint was going to an air show in Tulsa, and she'd heard him fly off not long ago. She decided this would be a good time to fulfill her promise to check out his building's plumbing. He wouldn't be around to clutter up her thoughts—as if his absence were any real help.

She peeked into the hangar and saw Sam sweeping the floor with a huge push broom. He seemed delighted with the job, and she had to smile. How many times had she asked him to sweep the kitchen, only to have him stare at her as if she had asked him to eat worms?

Bo had his back to her and was standing at a long, cluttered worktable at the back of the hangar. "Hi," she called into the cavernous room. Both heads lifted and waved as she walked toward them around the gleaming World War II plane. "Thought I'd come see how the other half lives."

"Pretty high. Pretty high," Bo said with a laugh. "We were just about to pop open some champagne."

Sam leaned on his push broom and grinned. "We're gonna change the Bearcat's spark plugs in a little while. Wanna help?"

She stopped beside him and brushed hair from his eyes. "I'd love to, but I promised Mr. McCord I'd check out his plumbing, and this is the first chance I've had." It was a small lie, but it would probably go unnoticed.

"Oh, okay."

Sam went back to his sweeping, and Lorna walked over to Bo, who was wearing his usual greasy coveralls. He was wiping his hands with a rag. "Don't see much of you these days," she said. "How's Maggie?"

He turned to her, and his red beard split in a charmingly lovesick grin. "She's fine and dandy. If you'd come by the diner at lunch from time to time, you'd see her."

Lorna felt her cheeks get hot, but tried to shrug off his remark. "Busy becoming a millionaire."

"Yeah, I know you're busy."

"Tell the girls I'll try to make it next week." Her glance roamed over the workbench, which was scattered with tools and engine parts, finally falling on a metal box exactly like her recipe holder. She picked it up. "What are you, Bo the Gourmet Mechanic?"

He shook his head. "I wish. Nope, that's Clint's stunt box."

She was puzzled. "What's a stunt box?"

"Those cards are for when he's learning a new stunt. He writes every maneuver down on a four-by-eight card and tapes it to his control console. Then he practices the stunt at high altitude until he knows it down to the smallest detail. He's one damned careful son of a gun. Like he says, when you're flying two hundred miles per hour fifteen feet off the ground, you can't drop your concentration for even a second. He's gotta know exactly what he's doing."

Curious, she set down her tool case and opened the box and thumbed through the cards. Sure enough, there were figures, angles, drawings and more figures, all done in a firm, precise hand. What was written down was Greek to her, but it was clear that each card contained detailed outlines of stunts that looked completely death-defying when seen in the air. "I thought he took dares from the audience," she mused, not realizing she'd spoken aloud until she heard her voice.

Bo took up his hand-wiping again. "Sure. But all those things they dare him to do, he's already done a thousand times before. The man's a pro." He shrugged his huge shoulders. "There's a sayin' in his line of work that goes, 'There are no old, *bold* pilots.' Clint lives by that sayin'. He tells the announcer to hold the real crazy dares till last and then say they're out of time. He's been doing this for a lot of years. He's no fool."

She thought about that for a second, then murmured, "And I said he was nuts."

His good-natured laugh brought her head up with a jerk. "Funny. He said the same thing about you, just before he left."

She'd replaced the card she'd taken out, but his comment stilled her before she closed the box. She peered at him, to discover he was looking at her, a quizzical smile on his face. She couldn't tell if Clint or Sam had mentioned the jelly bean bath or not, and decided she'd rather not discuss it. "Bo, do you think I'm more reckless than Clint?"

"I wouldn't really know about you, ma'am." He grunted, shrugging those mammoth shoulders. "But Clint, now, he's a real laid-back man—except when you're talking flying. There, everybody's more reckless than he is."

She absorbed his explanation with a contemplative frown. Had her opinion of Clint been warped by her experiences with Wild Bill? Now that she thought back, had she ever really seen Clint do one reckless thing—besides the stunts? Hadn't he taken meticulous phone messages for her? Wasn't his office an example of a well-organized, conservative mind? And wasn't he the one to remember to use condoms? Her heart flip-flopped at the memory of his lovemaking. Nothing conservative about that! Forcing her mind back to the subject, she asked softly, "Has he ever crashed?"

"Naw. Never came close. These planes are meant to handle stunt flying. He's had a couple of in-flight fires, but every pilot sees those sooner or later."

She picked up her toolbox, trying to distill this news. How could it be? The two notions seemed so opposite— the words *careful* and *barnstormer*.

"In September he's competing in Reno, Nevada, in the biggest air race in the country. That's why I'm getting the Bearcat here in tip-top shape. She's his race plane."

Lorna stared blankly at the fighter hulking silently in the hangar, still trying to absorb what Bo had told her. "A race? Not stunts?"

Bo leaned against the worktable. It creaked under his weight. "Yeah. It's a nine-mile course, where the racers fly fifty feet off the ground at five hundred miles an hour. The ten top dogs in that contest team up for the world competition. Nice trophy, too."

"World competition?"

"Yeah. He'll make it. It's gonna be in France this year. But that's Clint. Never settles down in one place for long."

She nodded, remembering the framed poem in his office. His code—breaking hearts and moving on. At least that was no surprise to her. "Well—I'd better get to work."

"Right. Me, too."

"You—you know him well, don't you?"

"Since we were kids. Why?"

She shook her head, smiling weakly. "Nothing." Her feet felt like lead weights as she walked away. So Clint wasn't as crazy as she'd believed him to be. He was a careful, probably even a *normal* man. Ironically, he was exactly the sort of guy she'd hoped to find in Brazen Gulch. It was too bad women were nothing but passing pleasures to him as he moved, and kept on moving.

She wondered why he was a vagabond, a man who couldn't put down roots and wouldn't commit to marriage. She stopped, looking over her shoulder. "Bo?"

Sam had walked to the workbench and was standing beside the big man. At the sound of her questioning voice, both of them turned to look at her. "Yes, ma'am?"

Regretting she'd said anything, she shrugged and turned away. "Never mind."

She bit her lower lip. She'd been about to ask if Bo knew why Clint was the way he was. Why he didn't want to settle down and get married. But she realized it didn't matter. That was the mistake so many women made about men. They thought they would be the one to change him. It was only later, when their hearts were broken, that they realized how wrong they'd been. People didn't change unless *they* wanted to. She'd learned that the hard way with Wild Bill.

No. Even after discovering Clint wasn't reckless, like Bill, she knew she'd done the right thing in calling off the affair before it was too late—before she'd fallen hopelessly in love. Reaching the door to the hangar bathroom, she leaned against it, feeling queasy. Who was she trying to kid with this bull? It had been too late for her heart the first time she saw the most brazen grin in Brazen Gulch.

Damn Clint McCord *and* his grin.

9

Lorna had gone all the way around the bend to Lame-brain Land—a land she had a feeling Disney wouldn't be interested in. It wasn't a fun place. But nothing else would explain why she was walking to Clint's office, knowing he was there, just because she had an overwhelming urge to see him. Just to *see* him! She knew their relationship had no future. But she needed to see him once more, to at least apologize for accusing him of having a death wish. That was what she hoped she planned to do, anyway.

She was carrying a little white bag. A peace offering. Another lamebrain idea, since it was full of leftover jelly beans. For some reason, she had to let him know why she'd been in a bathtub full of candy, her only companion one of the town's bachelors.

When she knocked on his office door, her heart was already blocking her throat. She just hoped she could talk when the time came.

"Come in."

The sound of his voice both thrilled and terrified her, making her heartbeat escalate to dangerous levels. Gathering her poise, she turned the knob and stepped inside the office. Clint looked up from his ledger and did a double take when he realized who it was. She smiled, but she was so nervous the effort hurt. "Hi," she said, a bit breath-less.

He scanned her with speculative eyes. "If it isn't Miss Bloodmobile." Looking down at his record book, he lifted his pencil, muttering, "I already gave, remember?"

She sucked in air. This was going badly. "I—I brought you something." Holding up the sack, she rattled it. "A gift."

He peered at her again, then leaned forward, resting his elbows on his desk. "What is it, a little llama?"

She felt her embattled composure under further attack at the reminder of when she'd given that speech—and what they'd done shortly afterward. Her smile faltered. "Uh—no. Jelly beans. Leftovers. I wanted to explain about what I was doing in the—"

"Sam told me."

She supposed she shouldn't be surprised. "Oh? About Miss Texas in the bathtub of jelly beans and the ten-thousand-dollar prize if anybody could guess the number of beans—"

"Sam told me," he repeated, his expression closed. "Including the fact that your body mass..." He paused, and it was almost as though the mention of her body caused him some pain. Or maybe not. She was so scared, she wasn't sure her brain was working properly. He cleared his throat and went on, "Your body mass came closest to Miss Texas's, except for twelve pounds. The reason for the bowling ball."

She nodded, swallowing with difficulty. "A good cause, don't you think?"

His eyebrows lifted in mild agreement, but there was no grin. His glance gravitated to the white bag as she placed it on his desk. "Thank you for the beans, Mrs. Willow. Is that all?"

She gritted her teeth. He was making this apology darned hard. She allowed her smile to fade. "Not quite."

He watched her, but said nothing.

She couldn't maintain eye contact, and found herself focusing on his hands. Nice hands. Short, clean nails. Long, tanned fingers. Talented and loving in the dark. They weren't fisted, just resting atop his open ledger. Why did he have to look so calm? Well, not calm, exactly, but distant. Yes, that was it. He was being purposefully distant.

She supposed she couldn't blame him. She'd pricked his ego by running off after—well, by running off. "Uh, I also wanted to say I'm sorry for calling you reckless. Bo told me how you practice your stunts and that you know what you're doing all the time. So..." She made herself look him in the face. "So, I'm sorry."

He appraised her with narrowed eyes. "And?"

She stared, confused by his question. "Well...and..." She stumbled around in her mind, not knowing what he expected. "I—just wanted you to know I'm sorry for jumping to that conclusion."

"Why are you telling me all this?" He sat back, his gaze probing. "Does any of it change your feelings about me sexually?"

She blanched, shocked by his candor. "Well...well, no. I...I still..."

"Then thanks again for the jelly beans." He lifted his pencil and leaned over his ledger, summarily dismissing her.

She was shocked by his rudeness. What had happened to his easy camaraderie? Why couldn't he let things go

back to the way they'd been? Why couldn't they just be
tenant and landlord again? "What are you saying?" she
asked, unable to hide the hurt in her voice. "What do you
mean, how does this change my feelings *sexually?*"

"You know what I mean." He glanced at her. "But if
you insist on a translation, here it is. I still want you, and
unless you want me, then give me a break and go away."

"You only want me like a little boy wants ice cream!"
she blurted, crushed by his attitude. "There's plenty more
out there where that came from, and don't tell me you
won't take full advantage of it! So, you give *me* a break!"

He didn't respond, but his jaw bunched with irritation.

"What is it with you? Haven't you ever been dumped?
Is your ego so colossal you can't believe a woman might
not sacrifice all her principles—her hopes and dreams—to
have you, however briefly?"

He peered her way, thumping the pencil down. His eyes
sparked with frustration. "Do you want me to say I love
you? Is that it? Do you want me to ask you to marry me?"

Her lips sagged open. *Did he read minds?* To save her
pride, she overreacted by madly shaking her head and
backing away. "Not in *this* life, Buster!"

"Good, because it won't happen." He vaulted up, tow-
ering there, glorious even in his anger. "Do you want to
know why I won't ask you?"

"No! It doesn't matter." Miscalculating the exit, she
slammed into the doorjamb, bumping her head. For a
moment she saw stars.

Apparently she winced, because his features registered
a shadow of worry. "Are you okay?"

She rubbed the back of her head. "Like you care."

His scowl deepened, but it seemed as though his ire dissipated somewhat. Planting the flat of his hands on the

desk, he lowered himself into his chair. "I suppose I owe you my thanks for the new trap on my kitchen sink."

She glared at him through dancing, dissolving stars. "I told you when I first moved in I'd take a look at your plumbing. Since you've kept things in good shape, you didn't need much work done." The admission was hard-fought, but she felt derelict that she'd stayed on his property for a month and all she'd repaid him with was one inexpensive part. "I'll do your plumbing for free for a year. Okay?"

"A fantasy come true," he mumbled, crossing his arms before him.

A fearful emptiness opened up inside her as she watched his expression again grow detached. Even his eyes cooled.

She sidestepped into the doorway. Just thinking about what she had to say next shattered her, but it needed to be finished, *now*. "One other thing. My place in town is ready. Sam and I are moving out of the cottage tomorrow."

He looked momentarily speechless with surprise. It unnerved her to watch his lean face, so solemn, yet so painfully handsome. The wayward lock of ebony hair grazed his brow just as it had the first time she'd seen him. It seemed to mock her, as if to say, *"You'll never touch me again, poor dear."*

He pursed his lips. As he did, his eyes caught the light of the setting sun and glimmered with false merriment. She missed that amused flicker and had to force back a sob at its loss. Yet the cruelest sadness that enveloped her heart came the instant she realized that the worst of it was, he didn't smile at her anymore.

After a tense few seconds, he nodded. "Good luck." Though he said it through thinned lips, he seemed to genuinely mean it.

She shrugged, praying it masked her despair. She was leaving the man she loved. A man who seemed to care about her, but for some reason couldn't commit. "Thanks..." she whispered, slipping out the door. It took every ounce of her strength to hold back her welling tears.

Matrimonially speaking, a lot was beginning to happen in Brazen Gulch. Wedding bells seemed almost deafening in the little town. During the two weeks since Lorna had moved into her apartment over the plumbing store, Reva had married Herm the toe-sucker, Joe-her-first-date had found his ladylove among the "hotel women," there had been three other weddings, and today, August 29, Bo was marrying Maggie.

As Lorna parked her truck near the quaint brick chapel, she looked at her watch. It was past seven-thirty. She'd already missed the seven-o'clock ceremony, but she'd made it for the reception. All in all, today had been rotten. It seemed like aliens had come down during the night and rendered every water heater in town inoperable. Suddenly, it was *Village of the Damned Water Heaters,* starring Lorna "Prunefoot" Willow. That nutty thought brought a smile; it was her first in some time.

The chapel was at the edge of town, on a treeless half-acre lot. From her elevated vantage point, she could see the green awning that had been set up in the side yard where the reception was being held. Beyond the church property was an endless stretch of barbed-wire fence, separating the fifty or sixty wedding guests from tall grasses, rolling tumbleweed and a cluster of curious cows.

Somehow, out here in the vastness of West Texas, the two diverse but friendly environments worked nicely together, and for the first time in a while she felt as if this move had been a good idea, after all. How many places could a cow enjoy a wedding?

Since it was warm, and neither Maggie nor Bo were "fancy" people, the ceremony had been casual. Lorna had decided to wear a yellow sundress, and for once she wasn't wearing her chunky boots. She'd finally had time to pick up some white sandals, and, much to Barney's dismay, she'd taken to keeping them in the refrigerator.

Gathering her full skirt, she hopped down from the cab of her truck as Sam came running up, a big grin splitting his face. He was in an oversize white shirt and loose black slacks. A yellow carnation was pinned to his chest. "Hi, Mom. Glad you finally got here. What happened?"

She kissed his cheek. "Water-heaters-from-heck day. How did it go being a groomsman?"

Her son took her hand and pulled her toward the guests milling about on the manicured grounds. "I didn't screw up once. Clint helped me."

"I knew you'd be perfect." She put an arm about his shoulder, trying to appear casual, though her stomach was knotting up. Clint had been Bo's best man, and she knew she'd have to see him. She'd managed to avoid running into him since she'd left the flying school. But she couldn't miss Maggie and Bo's wedding completely. So, today, she had no choice.

"Maggie said she was sure sorry you couldn't be her bridesmaid, but Reva and Thel made out okay."

"I'm glad."

"Why couldn't you, Mom?"

Lorna's smile faltered, but she kept her gaze trained on her son, preferring his searching expression to the alternative possibility of seeing Clint. She'd turned down Maggie's request, saying Maggie had spent more time with Thelma and Reva and they deserved the honor. She had had a feeling Maggie sensed there was something she wasn't saying, but she'd accepted Lorna's explanation with grace.

Realizing her son was staring at her, she refreshed her smile. "Oh...you know why I turned her down, Sam. Work. I would have hated to promise I'd be a bridesmaid and then not be there because of a plumbing emergency. Which is what happened."

"But Reva's a nurse. She coulda had an emergency."

Lorna laughed. "What are you, the district attorney?" She squeezed his shoulders. "I'm here now, and you know what? I feel like hugging Maggie and Bo."

He pointed toward the awning. "They're in the tent with the cake."

"Good. Sounds like I'm just in time for the eats."

Sam slung a thin arm about his mother's waist and laughed. "Some of us are going out for dinner after the receptacle."

"Reception." She tried not to frown at the possibility of who might be included in this dinner. "Have you already accepted?"

"Sure. It's mainly the wedding people—you know, ushers, bridesmaids, groomsmen and their families. You're my family."

Waving at acquaintances, she pestered the inside of her cheek. How was she going to get out of this darned dinner? She had no intention of spending the evening with Clint glowering at her.

She and Sam reached the awning, where a couple of card tables had been set up and covered with a white cloth. Lorna was relieved to see only Bo and Maggie standing there. A two-tiered cake sat before them. They'd just cut a couple of chunks from the top tier. Maggie stuffed some in Bo's mouth, smearing his cheek. Bo did the same thing to his new bride and Lorna smiled, clapping along with others who were watching or taking pictures.

"Lorna!" Maggie called, licking icing from her lips. "Come over here and give us a hug. Where have you been?"

For such a big woman, Maggie looked even more beautiful and feminine than ever. Of course, today she wasn't wearing jeans and a flannel shirt. Her strawberry-blond hair was cascading down her back in shiny, unadorned curls. Though she was wearing slacks and a manly shirt, they were white linen, and the blouse had a cutout of lace appliqué above the flap pockets. Lorna thought she looked perfect, considering her size and clothing preferences.

Bo was dressed very much like Sam, but he had a red rose pinned to his chest.

She rounded the table and received a bear hug from them both, unable to decide whose was more bone-crushing. "I'm happy for you two," she wheezed, stepping back and smiling. "Sorry about being late. Water heater emergency."

"Isn't that always the way!" Maggie kissed her cheek. "We'll forgive you if you'll cut cake for us." She held out the knife. "Bo and I have to go change out of these wedding duds."

Lorna accepted the cutlery with a grin. "I'm happy to serve."

"You heard Clint is giving us the cottage, since Bo's little room upstairs is mainly unfinished storage space and my place is a windowless stockroom."

Lorna had to work to hold on to her smile. "No, I hadn't heard. That's nice."

"It's just until we can build us a house," Bo said. "Maggie wants kids right away."

Lorna squeezed their hands. "Then you'd better get started," she joked. "I'll handle the cake."

With another excruciating hug, they were gone, and Lorna took up her duty as cake server.

She recognized Clint's hand as soon as he took one of the paper plates from the stack. A willful thrill shot up her spine like chain lightning. "Evening, Mrs. Willow," he murmured.

She continued to slice, hoping he hadn't spotted her momentary spasm. With trembly fingers, she lifted a piece and shifted it to his plate, praying it wouldn't tumble to the grass. Forcing her lips into the facsimile of a smile, she managed a breathless, "Hi..."

Tall and powerful, he stood there, looking devastating in his starched white shirt and trim black slacks. Avoiding his eyes, her glance drifted hungrily over him. He'd rolled up his sleeves, and she found herself searching for signs of scratches. There were none.

Her heart suffered damage at the unbidden rush of memories, and she tugged her gaze away. His hair was combed into place, but for that one lock, which stroked his forehead in the early-evening breeze. Finally, unable to help it, she reluctantly connected with his eyes. He was regarding her silently, his glance displaying none of the rancor she expected. "You look very nice," he said. Then he smiled, but the teasing quality was absent.

"Thank you." Her cheeks warmed and she felt her poise crack. Even his reserved smile made her crazy. Her gaze flitted behind him. The line was short, and nobody looked particularly irritated by the delay. But she knew standing there under Clint's tacit regard was doing her no good. Turning away, she placed the knife in the cake and made another cut. When she looked up, Clint was gone.

From that time on, she couldn't recall a single person who came through the line. Unfortunately, she registered where Clint was every minute, and to whom he talked. She was disgusted with herself for that.

"Mom?" Sam's voice drew her from her bizarre trance. "Maggie's going to throw the bouquet."

She looked around, noting she'd been slicing cake like a demon and nobody was even in line. "Okay, thanks, honey."

Together they walked to the front of the chapel, where there were six wooden steps that led inside. Maggie was standing at the top, in front of the arched double doors. Clad in green shorts and a matching blouse, she was waving a bouquet of white daisies and red rosebuds. "Okay, ladies. I know this isn't a hard town to find single guys in, but who wants to be next?"

There was a rousing cheer from the assembled women. When Lorna joined the group, she felt a hand on her arm. "Hi, Lorn!"

She turned to see Reva—now Mrs. Herman Toe-Sucker Humbolt. Her broad red lips were split in a smile. It was clear the woman had very happy feet. "I was afraid you weren't coming," she enthused, clutching her plump new husband with her other hand. "Better catch that bouquet. I recommend *m-a-r-r-i...*"

The rest of the spelling was drowned out by shrill cries as female guests grabbed for Maggie's bouquet.

"Oh, *Thel!*" Reva cried, delighted that her shy friend had caught the flowers, even though they'd been tossed directly into her face. Thelma's triumph had been more a case of self-defense than of athletic ability. Nevertheless, tradition had been satisfied. *"Thel!"* Reva yelled again, squeezing Lorna's arm and whispering loudly, "I predict she and Clyde will be hitched in a *m-o-n-t-h.*" Before Lorna could respond, the nurse hustled her husband off to congratulate Thelma on her good luck.

"Too bad, Mom," Sam said from her other side.

She looked at him, startled by his melancholy tone. "Honey... Do you want a daddy that badly?"

He shrugged skinny shoulders. "Naw. I just thought you might be lonely. You seem sorta—sad—lately."

Her heart dropped to her feet, and she knelt beside her son, taking his hands. "Oh, Sam, honey, I'm not sad." It was a lie, but what else could she say to him? It wasn't something a small boy could fix, no matter how sensible or diligent he might be. "How could I be sad when I have you?" She hugged him desperately.

He returned her hug. His seemed desperate, too, somehow. "Okay, Mom. But—but you could smile more."

She kissed his cheek, surreptitiously wiping her eyes. "I'll work on it."

"Ready for dinner, sport?"

Lorna stiffened as Sam withdrew from her arms. "I'm starved, Clint." He looked at his mother. "Ready, Mom?"

She reluctantly got to her feet. "I'm not really hungry. Why don't you go on?"

"Aw, Mom." Sam tugged at her hand. "Come on. It'll be fun."

She smiled at him. Though it began as an effort, her love for the boy spilled out, making the expression genuine. "Thanks, honey. But I'm pretty tired. Besides, since I was late to the wedding, I should help clean up. Go on and have a nice time."

She made herself look in Clint's direction, but focused over his shoulder. "I'll give you some money for Sam's meal. Let me get my purse."

As she turned toward the awning, he halted her with a hand at her wrist. His touch was incendiary, and she grew weak, her breath going out in a rush. "Don't," he said. "I want to do this."

She tugged on his grasp, failing in her bid for freedom. Okay, so she didn't try very hard. "Fine," she murmured. "Just drop him off at my place afterward."

"I would never have thought of that."

Sarcasm was rich in his tone, and she felt chastened. Before she could counsel herself about the foolishness of her act, she was facing him. His gaze drew hers, his dusky eyes compelling, erotic, *unfair*. He was daring her to resist him. He knew his power, and they both knew there was something chemical between them that was almost impossible to deny.

The bum was worldly enough to sense that it wouldn't take much to get her back in his bed. So far, he'd merely touched her arm, looked at her, and she was already trembling with longing. Oh, he was good. Not good for *her*, but very, very good.

"I'm not hungry," she insisted thickly.

He lifted a skeptical eyebrow. "I think you are."

She blanched at his sly double entendre, snatching her hand from his grip. "Sam, could you go get my purse?"

"But, Mom, Clint said he wanted—"

"I need to powder my nose." She canted her head toward the awning. "Please, honey?"

His expression indicated that he took her request at face value, and he sprinted off. As soon as he was out of earshot, she glared at Clint. "This isn't about dinner, is it? I thought you told me to stay away from you!"

He looked away, his jaw shifting left, then right, as though he were irritated, or nervous, or both. When his glance touched hers again, he still hesitated, as if measuring his words. "I want you back, Lorna," he said, very quietly.

She stared at him, stunned. Against her better judgment, her heart took a hopeful leap. "What do you mean?"

"I mean I want you back, dammit!" The words came out impatiently, tenderness and affliction in his eyes. "It's driving me crazy to think of you with other men." He took her hands in his big, warm ones. "Why can't we be together?"

She searched fervently for the meaning behind his words. Was he proposing marriage? Some nagging little voice in her brain was telling her not to get her hopes up. "On what terms would we be together?" she asked, hardly able to squeeze the question past her paralyzed throat.

"Terms?"

She nodded stiffly. "Terms. Like—for how long?"

He cursed under his breath. Clearly, he didn't make it a practice of crawling to a woman. Nostrils flaring, he drew a step nearer. Now they were close enough to kiss. It would only take a slight lowering of his head or a lifting of her chin to complete the deed. "Lorna, I promise you all I have to give for as long as it lasts."

All I have to give for as long as it lasts.

Her brain took in the jumble of words and tried to form them into a proposal of marriage. But no matter how she composed them and recomposed them, she got nothing that smacked of permanence. He was still the same man who broke hearts and roamed the world at will. He'd told her once that he was obsessed with her. The words *love* and *forever* didn't seem to compute with him.

A raw, primal grief overwhelmed her, and she grew angry with herself that she'd let him draw her back under his spell, even for a moment. She'd known deep in her soul that a brief affair was all he would ever offer. Her lips parted slightly, but not for a kiss. She had so much she wanted to shout at him, but she couldn't find the strength.

"Lorna?" he coaxed, moving a hair closer.

Suddenly she sensed he was actually going to kiss her, and she didn't dare allow that. Not here. *Not ever.* Knowing she couldn't just stand like a stone monument to hurt and despair, she choked out a bitter laugh. "Let me get this straight. Your offer is for us to have sex until you get bored? How romantic." Yanking free from his grasp, she backed to a safer distance. "Believe it or not, I've had that offer before."

Sam came rushing up, holding her purse aloft. "Here it is."

She spun around and grabbed it. *"Thanks!"* The word came out like a growl, but she was much too upset to worry about that now.

"You okay, Mom?" Sam called as she stomped away.

"Let her go," Clint murmured.

Her mind screamed back, *Follow your own advice, Mr. McCord, and leave my heart alone!*

* * *

Lorna was a nervous wreck. Why had she volunteered to help with that jelly bean thing? Who would have thought they'd actually win the ten thousand dollars? And now, to celebrate, the town was having an appreciation barbecue and street dance in her honor. She dropped her head into her hands, moaning. Everybody in town would be there to witness her mortification.

Well, maybe not everybody. It was September 8, the last week of summer before school started. Since it was Friday night, that probably meant Clint would be off at an air show. She prayed he was in St. Louis or Miami. Somewhere very far away. Being near him hurt too much.

She checked her watch. Nearly six o'clock. Where was Sam? It was one of the other mothers' turns at camp carpool, but usually he was home by 5:15. Hurrying to the telephone table beside the sofa, she opened the drawer to check the carpool phone list. Just as she began to dial, the door banged open and Sam spilled inside.

"Sorry I'm late, but everybody in camp went out to the airfield this afternoon for a special last-day surprise. Clint did us a show. It was killer!" He plopped on the beige sofa. "My favorite trick was when he went zooming down the runway sideways." He hopped up and spread his arms to mimic an airplane. Bending over so one hand almost touched the multicolored rug and the other pointed toward the ceiling, he ran across the room. "He flew this way. One wing was like two inches off the ground! It was totally *awe*some!"

Relief at seeing her son was mixed with high anxiety at having to listen to him praise Clint. She replaced the phone's receiver in its cradle as he continued to talk about the impromptu air show.

"And then he got in the Bearcat and showed us how he's going to race next week. He flew really, really fast and low. There was a big crowd out there, all cheering. He was *stupid phat!*" He paused and looked up, apparently judging her expression for signs of adult bewilderment. "*Stupid phat* means *really good,* you know."

She rolled her eyes. "This week, it means really good. Next week it'll go back to describing my thighs."

He laughed, then went on telling her how stupid-phat-awesome-bad-killer Clint was. She listened with tightly clamped jaws until he took a breath, and then she cut in. "Honey, you need to get cleaned up. The barbecue starts in a few minutes."

"Okay, sure." He hustled to a bureau and grabbed clean underwear and headed through her bedroom into the bath. "I'll be ready."

She nodded, but to thin air. Feeling a little feeble, she sat down heavily on the couch. So Clint was in town after all.

Fifteen minutes later, they set out on the two-block walk to where the street dance and barbecue were being held. Lorna felt like a fraud. She didn't deserve to be honored just because she was *about* the same size as Miss Texas. They might as well honor the bowling ball. But Mayor Coffee and the scout leader had disagreed. So tonight was Lorna Willow Night in Brazen Gulch.

A rock band was set up on the sidewalk outside the sheriff's office, their electrical cords snaking inside the building. Even from two blocks away, the music was deafening.

"Killer. It's *loud!*" Sam said, running on ahead.

"Wait, honey..." she called, then let it go. He was so excited, she didn't want to dampen his enthusiasm. All his camp friends would be there, and this was his first grown-up party. Besides, he was a celebrity of sorts, being the son of Lorna Willow Night. She grinned after him as he deserted her. Kids.

She scanned the muscled and tattooed members of the rock band when she passed. The bass drum was emblazoned with a lightning-strike scribble: The Backhoe Babe Chasers. None of them looked familiar, and she was surprised. She figured she'd been out with most of the babe chasers in town by now.

There were people everywhere. Like ants on a discarded hamburger. It looked and sounded like a county fair. Even smelled that way, with the aroma of charcoaling beef ribs and hot dogs, and the long lines of tables weighted down with everything from taco salad to rhubarb cake.

As she strolled, she saw lots of people she knew, people whose plumbing she knew even more intimately. She didn't see Clint, however. As time passed, she became more and more relieved. Maybe he'd left for an air show, after all.

At seven-thirty, when everyone was groaning about being stuffed to the gills, the ceremony she dreaded began. It took place in the vacant lot beside the sheriff's office. Lorna was embarrassed when she was called to the wooden platform constructed for the evening, to stand before the scout troop and Udell.

Mayor Coffee, ever florid, ever fingering his bolo, grinned broadly at her as he offered his beefy hand to assist her up. She'd been so disconcerted she was being venerated for her "body mass," she'd opted to wear a loose-fitting dress that flowed to her ankles. She had no intention of showing off her *body mass*. It was bad enough that the words had to be blared out over a loudspeaker.

As Lorna endured the ordeal with a pasted-on grin, she was startled to discover that the ten thousand dollars would be used to turn this vacant lot into a little park with a fountain.

"And in honor of this valiant citizen who gave of herself for this worthy project, the park will be called Lorna Willow Square."

Amid whistles and applause, she blanched at the overkill of attention. After thanking the mayor and the scout troop, she made a hasty exit from the stage. Luckily, the Backhoe Babe Chasers burst into a loud version of Prince's "Little Red Corvette," making it difficult for well-wishers to talk. Very soon, most of Brazen Gulch was wriggling and cavorting in the street as the dance began in earnest.

With a heavy exhalation, Lorna decided to try to find Sam and go home. She'd had about all the notoriety she could cope with for one evening. She walked around, looking for her skinny blond boy. As her glance passed over the dancers, she noticed Bo and Maggie clasped together in the middle of the street. The Babe Chasers were now playing "The Greatest Love of All," an inspiring, sexy melody, even in the hands of *this* band. Couples were plastered together all along the block. It was as though there'd been a little earthquake and people had grabbed at each other to keep from falling.

She shook her head at herself. Maybe it had been too long since she'd felt like those couples. Squeezing her eyes shut, she had to admit the truth—it hadn't been long at all. But knowing there could never be anything between Clint and her had filled her with such a lonely, wretched sadness, her mind had to work day and night to minimize the importance of the soft emotions that made people want to be close.

Despondent, she spun away from the view, then stumbled to a halt. *He* was standing there. Her breathing stopped as dark, earnest eyes sought hers. "I think this is our dance," he said, drawing her into his arms.

Oh, Lord. It was ridiculous how quickly she melted when he was close. She fought the feeling. "No, I—I have to find Sam."

He didn't let her go. On the contrary, he began to move with her to the music. "Sam's in front of the barbershop, winning the ice-cream-eating contest."

She shifted to look behind him. Sure enough, half a block away, there he was. His face and shirt were horrible messes, but he looked as if he were having fun.

Clint's chuckle drew her back. "He's a talented kid."

His fingers splayed, moving down her back to hold her more firmly against him. The warmth of his embrace was exhilarating. His scent enveloped her in a mist of uninvited desire. How quickly he could turn her resolve to mush! "Don't—don't do this, Clint."

He bent his head toward her. She could feel his breath on her face. "Don't do what?" His lips brushed her cheek.

She closed her eyes, hating herself for relishing his nearness. Unwillingly, she found herself swaying to the seductive strains, their bodies as one. Darkness was falling and, sadly, so was she.

"I don't want to dance with you," she whimpered helplessly.

"I know. Just give me until the song's over."

She swallowed hard. "Why aren't you at an air show somewhere?"

"I don't have anything more until the race."

"Oh—yes." She couldn't help but look up into his face. "How dangerous is it—really?"

He shrugged beneath the hand she'd tentatively placed on his shoulder. "Not very—if I don't lose my concentration."

His nearness, his woodsy scent, his soft voice, were like a narcotic, lulling her into a hazardous state of euphoria. His gaze caressed her face, moving closer. "Don't," she pleaded. Her entreaty had a double meaning, for she sensed he was going to kiss her.

He straightened slightly, his lips parting in a wry grin. "I lost my head."

Misery twisted her insides. She loved him so much. She didn't want him to be hurt—or even killed—in a plane crash. Couldn't stand the idea of never seeing him again. Without thinking about the right or wrong of it, she whispered, "Be careful."

His glance shifted away, and he didn't answer. She watched him, scanned his face in the gloaming. His brilliant black eyes were fixed on the sun as it set. His jaw worked.

What was he thinking? She could tell by the crease of his brow that he cared for her, that he was fighting some internal battle. Oh, Lord, she was a weak woman. Here she was, all of a sudden thinking she'd been too hasty in rejecting him so completely. Maybe all he needed was a little time to face his demons and defeat them. Maybe there was still hope for a future for them.

Out of the blue, she was so disconcerted she didn't know what to do. She didn't know what was right anymore. She bit her lower lip, needing to tell him how desperately she loved him, that she would give him all the time he needed, all the time she had left in the world, if that was what it took.

As the music changed to something faster, the bothersome little voice in her head was raging at her, telling her what a spineless fool she was, but she refused to listen anymore. She loved him, would always love him. "Clint—"

"I know," he said, his tone grudging. "My dance is over." When he looked at her, his expression was serious, his half smile touched by sadness. "I just wanted to say goodbye. I'm leaving Brazen Gulch."

10

Clint watched her luminous eyes widen as her body tensed under his fingers. Her astonishment was genuine, and he was a little surprised. "Didn't you expect this of me, sooner or later?"

She recovered quickly and a smile trembled to her lips. He winced inwardly. She wasn't fooling him; he'd hurt her, he could tell. She cared about him. No woman could make love with the uninhibited passion she'd shown if it was only sex to her.

Hell, he'd hurt women before when he left them, but never had he felt the pain in his own heart. But he couldn't settle down, and she wouldn't settle for what he could offer her. So it was better that he leave now, and quit torturing them both.

"Sure—I knew you'd go," she mumbled finally, her voice tight. "I just—forgot for a minute." Pulling from his grasp, she stepped back. "Good luck in the race, Clint." Looking away hastily, she ran both hands through her hair. "Well, I—I think I'll go see how Sam's doing."

"Before you go..." He wondered why in the hell he was detaining her, but he had to say something positive. "I hope you find your Andy of Mayberry."

When she looked back at him, her proud little chin tilted upward, and her eyes glistened in the dim light. "I've got to go." She spun toward the barbershop, where the contest was ending.

Well, *hell,* that was a jackass-stupid thing to say. He exhaled, grimacing. His only excuse was, he was hurting too. His glance flicked to Sam. Even his blond hair was streaked with chocolate. His face dripped with the stuff and his shirt was ruined, but he was grinning broadly, accepting an envelope. Apparently he'd won the free movie passes. Clint clapped for the boy, but his gaze drifted to Lorna.

Watching her stiff-backed retreat, he lost his smile. Streetlights all along the boulevard came on. Reluctantly he turned his back on the defiant sway of her hips, pretending to watch the dancers two-step to "Achy Breaky Heart."

Stuffing his hands in his pockets, he mused about how appropriate that tune was. He felt like crap inside, and there was an odd coldness running through his veins. It was a damn good thing he was leaving. He had a feeling if he stayed much longer he wouldn't be able to go.

And that would be hell on earth. His dream would be crushed, like his father's had been. Fear gripped him as he recalled the barrenness of his childhood. Growing up in a house where bitterness and resentment were living, pulsating entities—like a black hole, sucking up any possibility of happiness.

As a young man, his father had loved to fly more than anything and had wanted to be a barnstormer. But he'd been in love with a woman, too, and after they were married, she had told him she couldn't leave her tiny hometown, her family. And she couldn't bear to have him be away from home while he traveled to air shows. So, for his young bride, Clint's father gave up his dream and became a crop duster. The only joy left to him had been teaching his son to fly. Clint had loved it, too.

As he grew, he'd watched his father lose the best part of himself because of what he'd given up. His father had become more and more bitter in his loss. His grief had spread through the family like a sickness, killing everything beautiful and loving they might have had. Clint's mother had been miserable, too. Blaming her husband for her misery—never seeing her own tragic responsibility in it all.

Yes, families were a trap. Clint had learned that lesson early and well. His father had warned him time and again not to let anything—or anyone—stand in the way of his dreams. So, at sixteen, Clint had left the dysfunctional mess he'd called his family, to live out that dream—to roam the world, never to stay still. Never to allow his soul to shrivel and die the way he'd seen his father's die.

Nothing had threatened that dream until the day a bizarre blue fire truck pulled into his parking lot, and a woman with a squirrel on her head told him to go to hell with a proud lift of her chin.

"Hi, Clint," a young woman called, breaking through his dark musings. He glanced her way, recognizing her as someone he'd taken flying a week or so ago. Cute blonde, but he couldn't recall her name.

"Wanna dance, Clint? I just love to two-step."

Though a blistering weight burned his gut, he shrugged easily. "Why not, sweetheart?" Grinning down at her, he led her into the street. As they joined the others, he told himself again that it was best that he was leaving Brazen Gulch.

And none too soon.

* * *

It was the middle of September, and the month was dragging by. Lorna stared down at the newspaper in the cab of her truck. Clint's face mocked her from beneath the banner headline: Local Man Wins America's Biggest Air Race. He was holding a huge trophy, and grinning that grin she both hated and longed to see again.

Was it really any big shock to her that he'd won? That he was completely fine? Exhaling tiredly, she was sure he was a very contented man at this moment. She licked her lips in agitation, pulling her gaze from his face. She would have tossed out the paper by now, but there was a recipe inside that she wanted to keep.

Annoyed with herself, she flipped it over. Who was she trying to kid? Why was she carrying the darned thing around in her truck, then, if she just wanted to save one simple recipe? Did she plan to whip up the tuna loaf while she fixed Orville's leaky valve? *Sure,* she told herself sarcastically. *While I'm at it, why don't I sell myself some Florida swampland, too?*

She was parked in front of the diner. Before getting out, she checked her watch for the hundredth time. Noon, exactly. Clint would be getting back into town about now. Maggie had told her the city fathers planned a reception for their conquering ace out at his place, to cheer him home with a hero's welcome. Even the town's nine-person marching band would be there, blaring out their congratulations. She supposed he deserved the tribute, even if he wasn't going to be a "local man" much longer.

Sam dropped by the hangar most days after school, to see his friend Bo. Yesterday he'd come home with the news that a couple of Clint's flying buddies had flown out to look the place over, and that one of them was pretty set on buying it. Clint was just coming back to wrap things up before leaving for Europe.

She shook off the gloomy thought, grabbing her toolbox and sliding out of the cab. The best thing she could do for herself was to put Clint from her mind and get on with her life. Someday—maybe—her heart would heal enough for her to start looking for Andy of Mayberry, again. She'd just have to go on living and raising her son until that time came. If it did.

She tromped inside Orville's Diner. The place was empty, except for Mavis, straddling a stool at the counter and sipping coffee. She looked up, and when she recognized Lorna, she smiled. "Hi, hon!" She hopped down, and Lorna wondered how the woman maneuvered so well in such a tight uniform and spike heels. "Town's dead today." She shrugged. "Thanks to Sugar Hips Clint, my poor feet are gettin' a rest." She chomped her gum, beckoning. "Come on. I'll show you where the leak is. Orville's takin' his usual hour break in the can. Do you need to turn off the water?"

"Not just to tighten a leaky valve."

"Yeah. I didn't think it was a big deal." She shook her cheddar-cheese head. "Orville's a baby when it comes to tools. That thing's been leaking down in the basement for six months. Just in the last week it's got so bad, I have to keep traipsing down there every hour to change the bucket. And, hon, I ain't got the time. So I told Orville, either he got you over here or I was quittin'."

Lorna followed her down the stairs to the basement. "Orville wouldn't want to lose you."

"You bet your buttons." She stopped on the bottom step and looked back. "Old guy'd be nuts. Truckers come outta their way to eat here because of *me*." She laughed, then winked.

Lorna grinned and decided no comment was necessary. She pointed to a rusty bucket that had been placed beneath a pipe that came through the basement wall about four feet from the floor. "Is that the leak, over in that corner?"

"That's the sucker." She waved toward the washer and dryer, not far away. "Be careful. Orville spilled detergent down here last week. I swept most of it up, but it left a scum I ain't had time to get to yet."

"Thanks."

Lorna scanned the room. The basement wasn't big. Not much more than a gray concrete-block laundry room. It smelled of must and detergent. The only light was a bare hundred-watt bulb fastened to a rafter, but it was plenty to see with.

"If you need me or Orville, just yell." Mavis wiggled up the steps and disappeared into the diner.

Lorna walked to the leaky valve, set down her toolbox and opened it, picking out a wrench. Maybe she'd have time to eat lunch after all. This wouldn't take long.

She fitted the tool around the valve and turned it. There was a creaking sound, then a pop. It wasn't supposed to do that. It was then that she noticed the crack. *Defective.* In the split second it took for that thought to flash a warning in her brain, the valve broke and water spewed in her face. The force was strong enough to stun her, and she fell backward, gagging and choking.

She knew where the shutoff valve was. She'd seen it on the other side of the washer and dryer. All she had to do was get there. She scrambled to her feet, but as water mixed with detergent residue, the floor became like an ice rink, and she skidded, instinctively grabbing the pipe to keep from falling. When she did, her weight caused the pipe to twist, allowing water to cascade more freely—right down the bib of her coveralls. Since her pants were tucked into her waterproof boots, she was filling up like a blowup doll. The weight of all that water dragged her down until she was directly beneath the torrent, slipping, sliding and taking a very cold, drenching shower.

She gagged, gasping for air. Water was rising. Something must be blocking the drain. She slipped and slid, then dropped to her knees, deciding to crawl to the shutoff, but the water knocked her backward, against the wall. She was sputtering and coughing, blocking her face from the worst of it, when suddenly it all stopped. No more flood over her head or into her clothes.

Sprawled on the floor, leaning against the wall, she swiped her hair out of her face. Blinking repeatedly, she thanked heaven that Orville or Mavis had had the presence of mind to shut off the water.

"Oh...thanks..." She coughed, shaking her head. "That was freaky. It never happened to me before. I'm..." Her vision clearer, she focused on her savior. What she saw stilled her, numbed her mind. "Clint?" she whispered in disbelief.

He looked devilishly handsome standing there, one hand on the shutoff, his nice boots becoming ruined in several inches of sudsy water. "No, *I'm* Clint," he told her, his eyes openly amused. "You're wet."

That *smile!* It was back. He was smiling *that* smile at her. She swallowed, able to do no more than stare. And shiver.

His eyebrows dipped. "You're cold."

When he began to slosh toward her, his grin no longer evident, she snapped out of her stupor and struggled to her feet, then winced.

"Are you hurt?"

She drooped against the wall, her right foot supporting her weight. "I guess I twisted my ankle." As he approached, he slipped, but regained his balance. "Be careful!" she cried. "There's soap all over the floor!"

"Oh? I thought you just liked to dance in the shower." When he grinned at her again, her heart tumbled foolishly.

Before she could compute what was happening, he'd lifted her into his arms and was sloshing toward the steps. She was a soppy mess, and was disconcerted that he would have to see her this way, since it would probably be the last time. She never had catastrophes at work like this. Never! Why did fate have to be so cruel as to let him, of all people, see her at her worst?

Even though it would have done her less emotional damage to grab a cluster of rattlesnakes, she grasped his shoulders. She'd given up trying to be intelligent where this man was concerned. No longer able to stand the suspense, she asked, "Why are you here? I thought there was a big celebration out at the airfield."

He stopped halfway up the steps and looked at her. "There was."

"And you left?"

He shrugged. "I think they followed me. Listen."

Perplexed, she lifted her face toward the open door. Sure enough, it sounded like distant cheering and band music. "They're in the street?"

He shrugged again. "Sounds like."

Pressing away from him, she stared. "And you decided you wanted lunch?"

He chuckled, then continued to walk with her up the steps. "No, I decided I'd had all the accolades and praise I could stomach. I was getting a raging ego."

She frowned, uncomprehending.

"So," he continued, sweeping her through the tables toward the exit, "I decided I needed a good dose of rejection. And who better to give me that than you?"

His nearness was so disturbing, so stimulating, so confusing, she was at a loss. What was he saying? It made no sense. "You came to see me?"

"I did."

"What—? I don't— How—how did you find me?"

The teasing laughter was back in his gaze, and it affected her all the way to her bones. "If you don't want to be found in a town of two thousand souls, don't drive a bright blue fire truck."

He had a point, but her mind still reeled. "I'm afraid I'm lost."

"It must be catching," he murmured softly, only confusing her further.

When they emerged, there was a rousing cheer from the hundred or so spectators—even some scattered *oohs* and *aahs*. Clearly, the crowd hadn't expected Clint to be carrying a woman when he came out. Lorna hadn't expected it, either, and was in a state of paralysis. Still, she was out in the warm Texas sunshine. It felt good on her trembling body. She glanced around, blinking in bafflement at the smiling, expectant faces. "What—what do you want with me, Clint?"

His expression changed, his extraordinary eyes glowing with tenderness and strength of purpose. "I want you, Lorna," he whispered huskily. "I love you."

Her heart stopped beating, and the world no longer turned on its axis. The cheering crowd had gone still. No one spoke. No one moved. All of creation seemed to re-alize something significant had just happened.

"No..." she breathed, forcing herself not to read too much into his words. Surely he meant he wanted her *for now.* He loved her *for however long it lasted.*

Something stark and raw passed over his features, and then one corner of his mouth lifted in a resigned expres-sion. "That should take care of my ego."

He thought she was rejecting him? She shook her head, squeezing his shoulders. That was not what she'd meant at all. She knew now that she could never reject him. Could no longer deny the way she felt. "But—but you said you were leaving town."

He chuckled without mirth. "I know. I had a dream I had to live." She shivered violently, so he set her on the fender of her truck, and quickly shrugged out of his shirt, wrapping it about her shoulders. He was gorgeous, stand-ing there half-naked, his deep, somber gaze so full of pas-sion and sadness. "When I won that damned race, and it wasn't a kick anymore, I understood for the first time it wasn't *my* dream I've been living for the past twenty years. It was my father's."

He tugged the shirt closer around her. They were at eye level, and his features were riveting in their gentle beauty. "I think I've lived his dream long enough, don't you? It's time for me to get on with mine."

A wave of wild hope engulfed her. Was he talking about her? She didn't dare even think he meant permanence—even *marriage.* But she had to ask. "And...what is your dream?"

He shook his head, looking charmingly vulnerable. It was a captivating sight in such a virile, commanding man. "My dream is you, Lorna," he vowed quietly. "And Sam. Don't you see? I want to eat spinach meat loaf and have a hedgehog napping on my desk. I want to wear one blue sock and one brown sock because a squirrel has stolen their mates. I want to fight over the TV remote with llamas." His smile reappeared, but it was soft, loving. "I want you to marry me, and I want to have blond, curly-headed babies with you." His voice was hushed and rough with emotion. "That's my dream, Lorna. Is it too much to ask?"

Suddenly she felt no chill at all. How could she be cold, with such loving warmth radiating all around her? Tentatively she touched the stray lock of hair on his brow. She'd wanted this so badly for so long, she was having a hard time comprehending her good fortune. "You really mean it? You're not leaving?"

He made gentle love to her with his eyes. "How can I? Everything I love is here."

Her throat closed. "Clint..." she whispered. "I love you so much."

She was shocked when his eyes filled with a tender shimmering. Taking her face in his big, warm hands, he drew her lips to his. When they kissed, a cheer went up, and the two lovers separated slightly, having forgotten about their rapt audience. They shared embarrassed smiles, and he lifted her off the hood of her truck, murmuring, "I think you should get out of those wet things."

She nestled against him. "I do, too."

"I'll help."

She nuzzled his jaw, feeling a lightheartedness she'd never known before. "I dare you," she teased.

His rich chuckle rumbled pleasantly through her body.

She had a jarring thought. "What about Orville's water?"

"He needs a day off."

She hugged him, smiling. "Happy holiday, Orville."

Lorna knew Clint loved her, for she'd seen the truth glowing in his eyes. But she also understood that he would always love to fly. Because of his father's lost dream, he'd turned barnstorming into a symbol of freedom and happiness. At last—all on his own—he'd discovered that "roaming the world at will" had never been his dream at all. And that roaming—unfettered by love—was not really being free, just being alone.

So today was a red-letter day in Brazen Gulch. The little West Texas town had gained a plumber who no longer felt the need to clip her own wings, and a flyer whose passion could be satisfied in a much more earthy way—on solid ground—than he'd ever dreamed.

"Clint," Lorna whispered later, in the tangle of her sheets. "Do you like summer weddings or winter weddings?"

He kissed the tip of her nose. "How about day-after-tomorrow weddings?"

She snuggled in the crook of his arm. "I love those."

"By the way…" He ran a questing hand along her thigh. "Shouldn't Sam be coming home from school soon?"

"He's sleeping over at Mac Healy's."

His fingers dipped into a very feminine valley. "I love it when he does that."

"Mmmmm…" She sighed. "I love it when you do *that*…."

* * * * *

Coming in August from
Yours Truly™

BLIND-DATE BRIDE
by Lori Herter

Book 2 of Lori's exciting
Million-Dollar Marriages miniseries

Waitress Cheri Weatherwax had been offered the
deal of a lifetime. All she had to do was marry
Mr. Jake Derring, brilliant scientist, for one year
to receive one million dollars!

But when she stepped up to the altar and met her
groom, she suddenly forgot her lines. What was it she
was supposed to say to Mr. Tall, Dark and Handsome?

I guess...I think...I will?

**Million-Dollar Marriages: Lori Herter's
irresistible miniseries about saying "I do!"**

Only from

SILHOUETTE YOURS TRULY™
™

Love—when you least expect it!

Look us up on-line at: http://www.romance.net

LHMILLION-1

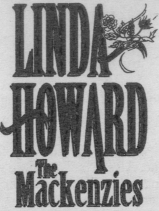

The exciting new cross-line continuity series about love, marriage—and Daddy's unexpected need for a baby carriage!

It all began with *THE BABY NOTION*
by Dixie Browning (Desire #1011 7/96)

And the romance in New Hope, Texas, continues with:

BABY IN A BASKET
by Helen R. Myers (Romance #1169 8/96)

Confirmed bachelor Mitch McCord finds a baby on his doorstep and turns to lovely gal-next-door Jenny Stevens for some lessons in fatherhood—and love!

Don't miss the upcoming books in this wonderful series:

MARRIED...WITH TWINS!
by Jennifer Mikels (Special Edition#1054, 9/96)

HOW TO HOOK A HUSBAND (AND A BABY)
by Carolyn Zane (Yours Truly #29, 10/96)

DISCOVERED: DADDY
by Marilyn Pappano (Intimate Moments #746, 11/96)

DADDY KNOWS LAST continues
each month...only from

Silhouette®

Look us up on-line at: http://www.romance.net

DKL-R

You can run, but you cannot hide...from love.

This August, experience danger, excitement and love on the run with three couples thrown together by life-threatening circumstances.

Enjoy three complete stories by some of your favorite authors—all in one special collection!

THE PRINCESS AND THE PEA
by Kathleen Korbel

IN SAFEKEEPING
by Naomi Horton

FUGITIVE
by Emilie Richards

Available this August wherever books are sold.

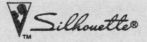

SREQ896

FORTUNE'S Children™

Bestselling Author

LISA JACKSON

Continues the twelve-book series—FORTUNE'S CHILDREN
in August 1996 with Book Two

THE MILLIONAIRE AND THE COWGIRL

When playboy millionaire Kyle Fortune inherited a Wyoming
ranch from his grandmother, he never expected to come
face-to-face with Samantha Rawlings, the willful woman
he'd never forgotten...and the daughter he'd never known.
Although Kyle enjoyed his jet-setting life-style, Samantha and
Caitlyn made him yearn for hearth and home.

MEET THE FORTUNES—a family whose legacy is greater than
riches. Because where there's a will...there's a *wedding!*

*A CASTING CALL TO
ALL FORTUNE'S CHILDREN FANS!*
If you are truly one of the fortunate
few, you may win a trip to
Los Angeles to audition for
Wheel of Fortune®. Look for
details in all retail Fortune's Children titles!

Look us up on-line at: http://www.romance.net

FC-2-C-R